The Tarot Saga: Prince Aaron's Fate

Andres Fragoso Jr

Published by Writers Sidekick Publishing, 2024.

This is a work of fiction. Similarities to real people, places, or events are entirely coincidental.

THE TAROT SAGA: PRINCE AARON'S FATE

First edition. November 17, 2024.

Copyright © 2024 Andres Fragoso Jr.

ISBN: 979-8230602071

Written by Andres Fragoso Jr.

Also by Andres Fragoso Jr

Las Vegas Authors Anthology 2019
Literary Visions Las Vegas Anthology 2020
In Isolation Getting Through COVID19 Anthology
Dominic's Guide to Text Codes Decoding the Confusing Language of Text Messaging
Listen, Poems on being Gay, Bipolar, and Alive
Under the Lemon Tree: a Family Recipe of Jealousy, Lies, and Betrayal
Loved Letters
Authors Portraits LV 2019, Anthology Showcasing Las Vegas Authors
Mica Shines Becoming a Drag King
Mica Shine's Becoming A Drag Queen
Mica Shine's Preparing For Drag
Mica Shine's The Right Cosmetics
Mica Shine's Wigs Styling
The Tarot Saga: Prince Aaron's Fate

Watch for more at andresfragosojr.com.

Table of Contents

The Awakening..1
Matt..5
Count Corvin 25
The Gypsy Queen 31
Prometheus 37
Mary Magdalen...43
Ashikaga Takauji 47
Hermes...53
The Tarot 57
The Reading 63
The Horoscope Reading..69
Position1 House of Identity 73
Position 2 House of Change 79
Position 3 House of Ideas 85
Position 4 House of Children 91
Position 5 House of Work 95
Position 6 House Of Love 99
Position 7 House of Family 105
Position 8 House of Magic 109
Position 9 House of Apprenticeship......................113
Position 10 House of Mental State 117
Position 11 House of Friends in Life 121
Position 12 House of Enemies 125
The Celtic Cross...129
Role of The Present Situation 133
Role of The Issue At Hand......................................137
Role of The Root Of The Issue 141
Role of The Recent Past Events 145
Role of The Best Solution 149
Role of The Next Step..153
Role of How You'll Deal..155
The Outcome...159
New Beginning..163

"In the cards lie our truths, our follies, our fates—But the hand that shuffles them is ours alone to guide."—Unknown Oracle

The Awakening

A chill of icy dread traced down my spine, dragging me from the depths of unconsciousness. My heavy eyelids lifted slowly, only to reveal a darkness so complete it felt like the shadows had woven themselves into a single, suffocating shroud.

An uneasy tension unfurled in my stomach while my limbs felt clumsy and weighed down. Tentatively, I extended my right arm, fingers brushing against a solid surface that felt both stone-like and disturbingly soft. I pressed harder, using the weight of my shoulder, but it was as immovable as fate itself.

Turning to my left, I encountered the same stoic resistance. My heartbeat spiked, my pulse driven by a manic burst of energy. I pushed forward, only for my forehead to collide painfully with a solid surface, cushioned yet unyielding. Claustrophobia seized me, squeezing out what remained of my rational thought. The grim truth settled in: I was trapped within a coffin.

Panic erupted like wildfire, consuming logic in its relentless flames. My breath came in shallow, frantic gasps. Yet, through my frenzy, a faint aroma of lavender drifted to my senses, oddly soothing in this confined prison. A ghostly sliver of reason returned. If the air held the scent of lavender, surely this coffin wasn't airtight.

Clinging to that aromatic thread, I strained my ears for any sound that might offer a clue. But the silence was absolute, swallowing even the faintest echo of my own breathing. I shut my eyes and began counting slowly, each number grounding me in reality. Trapped, yes, but still breathing, still conscious—still alive.

The subtle scent of cedar lingered in the stale air, earthy and rich as though the forest itself had lent its life to this chamber. Somewhere in the distance, rhythmic water droplets fell, each one punctuating the silence like a heartbeat.

I WAS BACK INSIDE THE old refrigerator, a rusted, cramped metal box tainted with the stench of mildew and rotting vegetables. "Help!" I screamed, sobbing in the darkness, gasping for air that grew thinner with every breath. Lightheaded and exhausted, I stopped crying, leaning my head to the side, waiting for death.

Eventually, my brother, Manuel, opened the door, laughing, pleased with his prank. Mother was nowhere nearby to console her seven-year-old, and Father was absent as well. Not that he would have punished Manuel, his favorite four-year-old son.

"THINK, THINK, THINK," I murmured, my voice barely audible yet reverberating in the confined space. My fingers trembled as I traced the edges of the interior, searching for any hope of escape. When they found a slight indent, I gripped it tightly and pushed it upward. A faint hiss rewarded my efforts, and the lid gave way just enough for a rush of icy air to fill my lungs.

My eyes adjusted quickly to the twilight sky, its muted blue light spilling into my velvet-lined prison. The air was rich with the scent of lavender mingling with a faint hint of a breeze, a strange blend that felt both calming and foreign. Beneath my bare feet, the marble floor was cool and unnervingly smooth, as if it had been meticulously crafted to belong in this very cell.

Clad in a thin red sarong, I stepped forward into the cell, shrouded in shadows and draped in the deepening twilight. A peculiar craving for dark chocolate struck me, sudden and overpowering. Baffled yet propelled by the urge, I ventured deeper into the cell. Every step felt like defiance, each breath a small victory against the lingering shadows of confinement.

As I moved, an image flickered in my mind: an old, overweight man sitting alone in a dim room, spooning chocolate ice cream into his mouth, trying to fill an empty void. I glanced down at my lean, muscular frame, a stark contrast to that spectral image, yet the hunger I felt wasn't for sustenance—it was an ache, an emotional chasm.

In visions, men drifted in and out, dismissive voices echoing phrases that stung like barbs: "If only you were a girl," or "Just wanted to see what it would be like." These words carved wounds in my self-worth, reducing me to an experiment, a fleeting thrill. Yet, in this present moment, I was free, and I focused on that freedom, on the cool breeze against my skin.

Through the dimness, my eyes caught a small, intricately carved box on a distant shelf. Inside, I knew, was a bar of the richest dark chocolate, saved for a moment of need. Yet, I hesitated, wary of it becoming yet another false comfort, like the spoonfuls of ice cream that never truly satisfied me.

AS MOONLIGHT STREAMED through a jagged crack above, I felt his presence. My Lord—a towering figure with raven-dark hair, most often tied in a careless ponytail, and eyes that glittered like onyx. His skin held a subtle luminescence as though bathed in lunar light, his all-black attire absorbing every hint of radiance.

The morning he placed me here, his breath brushed my skin, laced with lavender, and whispered words. "Tonight's festivities will see your past, present, and future with me." His cryptic promise lingered in my mind, each syllable biting against the cold.

Halloween was when I'd first met him, that one night when the boundaries between life and death wavered. Now, the faint sting of two small punctures on my neck drew me back to the present, each tender pulse an enigmatic invitation to explore the labyrinth of his world—and my own hidden past.

I LEANED AGAINST THE window's stone frame, fingers tracing its intricate carvings. Beneath me, the forest stretched out, a dark and inviting mystery. The moonlight spilled over a nearby lake, turning its surface into shimmering steps linking earth and sky.

From below, laughter and music drifted up, drawing my gaze to a gathering of revelers. Horseback riders adorned with autumn leaves and ribbons rode alongside decorated carriages, an eclectic crowd of artisans, musicians, and nobility mingling in colorful abandon. The aroma of cooking meats, freshly baked bread, and exotic dishes—eel, octopus—wafted through the air.

It struck me that this was the Halloween celebration my Lord had hinted at, an otherworldly affair in a castle I could hardly remember arriving at. Drawn to the revelry, I cast one last look at the moonlit landscape before turning from the window, eager to join this ancient celebration.

The scent of lavender, mingled with sage and the aged stone of the chamber, lent an air of antiquity and mystery. The absence of mirrors left me free of my own reflection—a respite I found oddly comforting.

The Van Gogh painting hanging on the wall added a warmth to the room that art alone could evoke, stirring memories of another place. I recalled my childhood room, a small, chaotic sanctuary smelling of detergent and city life. My mother's gentle smile as she brought me snacks, small gestures that had meant so much.

These memories, though distant, felt like a part of me, grounding me in a past that seemed a world away. Each space I inhabited—a coffin, a castle, a cluttered childhood room—served as a sanctuary for the various chapters of my life.

The lines between dream and reality blurred as I sat atop the coffin lid. The queen bed of my old room flashed in my mind, the soft cotton sheets, the comforting glow of a bedside lamp. My walls were once adorned with photos, art, and trinkets that mapped the person I was becoming. In my culture, a son didn't just leave; he waited until the family's wisdom declared him ready. My mother's voice echoed in my memory, "You'll leave when you're ready, Mijo."

Footsteps sounded down the corridor, pulling me back to the present. It was Matt, my valet, bringing a warmth that dispelled the chamber's chill. As he entered, his face was flushed with unease.

"Forgive me, My Prince," he said, his voice trembling. "Günter detained me in the dungeon—there was a trespasser on the grounds. He wanted me to witness the punishment."

My attention flickered between his words and the lingering cold in the room. An intruder could mean danger, but my immediate focus was on the urgency in Matt's voice.

"Light the fire," I commanded, "and tell me about this intruder."

Matt approached the fireplace, striking a match. As the flames took hold, warmth filled the room, illuminating his worn face. His voice steadied as he began recounting the night's events. As I listened, the scent of burning wood mingled with lavender and sage, blending into a foreboding yet comforting tapestry of ancient rituals and looming mysteries.

Matt

The air in the chamber was thick with tension, infused with the scent of aging parchment and wood oil from the creaking furniture. Low light flickered from the hearth, casting shifting shadows over Matt's face. Worn tapestries depicting ancient battles lined the walls, pressing inward like silent witnesses.

"It's alright," I said gently.

Matt's voice trembled. "The stables were a pretext," he began. "I was led down to where the sun's light never reaches, where damp walls crawl with moss, and every groan hangs in the air."

A chill spread through me. I had known of Günter's dark indulgences, but hearing them spoken aloud brought the castle's hidden cruelty into stark relief.

"I've seen it," Matt continued, voice barely more than a whisper. "He takes pleasure in it. He had a hammer, and I... I had to leave. I couldn't bear it anymore."

My chest tightened, anger coiling within me. This castle, under Count Corvin's rule, harbored unspeakable malice. The fire in the hearth crackled sharply as if sharing my fury. Yet, my authority did not extend to Günter; he answered only to the Count. I was hemmed in by titles and limitations, jurisdiction defined by bureaucracy.

But looking into Matt's eyes and seeing the pallor of his skin, I knew I could no longer ignore it. This wasn't just a matter of rank—it was a matter of decency, a vow to protect those within these walls. "I'll handle this," I said, infusing my voice with all the authority I could muster.

"Tonight marks a year since you joined us, My Prince," he said softly.

"It's hard to believe how swiftly time has passed."

Matt placed another log onto the fire, which caught quickly, hissing and popping as it surrendered to the flames. Straightening, he brushed soot from his palms. The firelight danced across his face, illuminating his golden hair, which fell in waves around his strong jawline. His eyes, an ocean-lit blue, caught the light. A flicker of something else appeared there before he looked away.

"Something on your mind, My Prince?" Matt asked, a small smile playing at the corner of his mouth, a slight imperfection that added a touch of youthfulness to his otherwise composed face. He moved about the room, lighting candles.

"Age creeps upon us, especially when we're not watching," I replied, tearing my gaze from him to the polished brass mantle where my reflection stared back. "But you, Matt, seem to have made a pact with time itself."

He chuckled, eyes still on the fire. "If only time were so easily swayed." His laughter blended with the crackle of the flames.

The steam rose as he poured hot water into the claw-foot tub in the corner. "Your bath is ready, My Prince."

I slipped off my robe and eased into the warm water. Matt approached, carrying a polished silver chalice. He poured a fragrant elixir into it.

"Drink this, My Prince."

I took the chalice, its cool metal a contrast to the warm water around me. "What's in it?"

"A blend of herbs from the castle's gardens—lemon balm for clarity, chamomile for calm, and a touch of mugwort for dreams yet to come."

I sipped, savoring the floral notes mingled with an earthy richness, like tasting a moonlit night. "It's wonderful."

Matt nodded. "It's an old family recipe, meant for times of transition."

"Transition. Is that what this is?" I placed the chalice on the tub's edge.

"Perhaps. Anniversaries aren't just for looking back but also for setting a course forward. Tonight could shape your future here."

I paused, absorbing his words. I studied him, noting the soft blush in his cheeks, the half-smile that creased the corner of his mouth. "Matt, do you ever wish for more? To attend a grand affair like tonight's not as a servant but as an honored guest?"

The question hung heavy in the air before he answered. "My Prince, my purpose and honor lie in serving you. There is joy in fulfilling my role."

"But if you could have any life, what would it be?" I pressed.

He turned, gazing out the window where the silk curtains stirred in the night breeze. "A different life?" he mused. "Perhaps I would be a scholar, studying ancient texts, or a healer like my ancestors, using my knowledge for the betterment of others."

I was touched by his honesty. "I hope one day you get to be all those things. You deserve more than to simply serve me."

He looked back and smiled. "As do you, My Prince. You deserve to be more than the sum of your past and the weight of your future."

"Matt, a firmer massage, if you would," I requested, setting a mood that matched the flickering candlelight around us.

"Of course, My Prince." His hands, warm and steady, pressed into the tension in my shoulders, and my thoughts drifted back to another night months ago when we had shared a moment in the library.

THE LIBRARY WAS INFUSED with the rich scent of worn leather and aged parchment. A crackling fire filled the room with a welcoming warmth, a sharp contrast to the chill emanating from the surrounding stone walls. From somewhere nearby, a distant hum of violins and woodwinds drifted in, musicians concealed in an adjacent chamber, filling the air with melodies that shifted from buoyant to somber.

Matt looked up from the chessboard, meeting my gaze as I poured a lush, sinful red wine into crystal goblets. "To rebellion," I toasted, and we laughed—a joyful, unrestrained sound bound to that room, to that singular hour.

We moved with the rhythm of the music, our laughter echoing through the chamber as the night blurred toward dawn. Ascending the grand staircase, our steps were light with wine and the thrill of unguarded freedom. Once within my chamber, we hovered at the edge of something both wondrous and perilous.

In the unearthly glow of twilight filtering through the heavy velvet drapes, I pulled him close, stopping just short of the eternal bond a vampire might bestow. Our lips met, not in hunger but in a sweet, lingering, audacious kiss. Laughing, we fell into my coffin, the sound filling the chamber as it rocked beneath us, nearly tipping over under the weight of our shared delight.

"WE ARE WHAT WE ARE, Matt," I said finally. "And some lines even I dare not cross."

He stilled, understanding etched in his gaze. We shared a silent agreement that night would remain unspoken, a memory tucked away beneath layers of duty.

"Are you well, My Prince?" Matt's voice pulled me from my thoughts. The air, still fragrant with rosewater and lavender, hung warmly around us. I blinked, refocusing on him.

"Yes, I'm ready to get out."

HE MOVED TO FETCH ME a towel, and my gaze drifted again to his attire. Ragged, worn nearly to threads, his clothes looked out of place amid the opulence of my private quarters. "Matt, why not wear a uniform like Günter or something else entirely? I always see you in the same worn clothes," I remarked.

Matt paused, holding the plush towel mid-air. "My Prince, Günter's family has been connected to Count Corvin since the castle was built. Their uniforms signify that lineage among the servants. I've only been by your side for a year. You never mentioned a need for me to wear a uniform or different clothing," he replied softly, his tone almost as if he were treading carefully around my pride.

His words hit me with a prick of guilt. "I hadn't realized it was within my authority. It's a revelation, really," I admitted, tasting the irony. Here I was, steeped in luxury, while Matt bore the appearance of deprivation. "This shall be rectified immediately."

Matt's eyes met mine, gleaming with a mixture of relief and humility. "You are my master. Your will is my command," he said, bowing his head slightly as if concealing his emotions behind a practiced humility.

"Being Master of this House is about responsibility as much as authority," I replied, feeling a new sense of determination take hold. "You'll have suitable attire. No more of this."

A subtle smile tugged at the corners of Matt's mouth. "Thank you, My Prince. Though...Günter might object," he added, his voice low, tinged with shyness, as if wary of disrupting the unspoken hierarchy.

"Günter's objections are of little concern to me," I declared, a quiet sense of satisfaction settling over me. "I'll deal with him. You need not worry."

My thoughts briefly flickered to Günter, his name a ridiculous mismatch to the severe man who bore it. It was like calling a wolf "Fluffy." I shook my head, dismissing the thought. That was a conflict for another day. Right now, there was a more pressing wrong to right—one that had endured far too long.

IT WAS EARLY DECEMBER, and Günter had led me down a dim, narrow corridor, the castle's heavy atmosphere pressing in around us—a blend of mildew, ancient wood, and lavender, perhaps meant to mask the castle's age. The air carried a haunting nostalgia. My boots echoed softly on the stone floors, and from above, the groan of timbers filled the silence as though the castle itself was speaking, laden with secrets.

"The Count has resided in New York since it was but untamed land," Günter had begun, his voice resonating in the cold hallway. "He's been master of this castle for generations. My family has served him for just as long."

We paused before an intricate tapestry that hung like a relic on the wall. Woven from silver, gold, and pigments too vivid to be natural, it displayed two genealogical trees interwoven as if bound by destiny. On one side was the lineage of Count Corvin, and on the other was that of the Günters.

"The fabric tells stories," Günter had said, brushing his fingers reverently over the tapestry's fine threads. "Look closely at the faces—my ancestors, growing old, changing. But the Count...observe him carefully. His visage remains unchanged. The same man, staring back through the ages."

I leaned in, squinting to examine the details. Just as Günter claimed, the faces in his lineage changed over time, some bearing a familial hump, others fairer or darker, growing old in the way all men do. But the Count's likeness was startlingly, arrogantly consistent.

"Are you saying," I hesitated, "that these are all Count Corvin? Not his ancestors?"

Günter turned to me, his eyes glimmering with an unreadable mix of pride and melancholy. "Believe, if you will, that my master is no ordinary man. We followed him across oceans through time itself. This castle was disassembled, stone by stone, and brought here from the Carpathian Mountains. We have served him since Plymouth Rock. Every wall, every tapestry is witness to his—and our—immortality."

The air around us seemed to grow colder, a chill that sent a shiver down my spine. As impossible as it sounded, as outlandish as it seemed, I felt the castle itself urging me to believe.

Yet, I couldn't. Immortality belonged to legends, not reality. "I find that hard to believe, Günter," I finally said, breaking the moment's eerie silence. "Ageless or not, no one escapes time."

Günter sighed as though my skepticism was all too familiar. "Belief is a fickle creature, my prince. But walls do talk, and so do tapestries. Someday, their tales may sound more plausible to you."

As we left the tapestries to their silent vigil, I felt an odd stirring—a sense that the walls, the groaning timbers, and even the air around me held secrets just beyond human understanding. For the first time, I began to question the boundaries of what I'd believed possible, feeling the seeds of doubt—or perhaps belief—taking root.

"MATT, HAVE YOU EVER left the castle or even ventured beyond the village?" I asked.

Matt hesitated, his gaze dropping briefly before meeting mine. "My Prince, stories have been passed down from my elders—warnings, really. They say those who leave the village are sometimes met with fates worse than we can imagine. In villages beyond ours, some serfs are less fortunate—beaten, starving, and even sold into slavery. The Count may be distant, but he is not cruel to us. We have roofs over our heads and food from the fields we tend. So long as we fulfill our duties, we live with a semblance of peace."

The room around us was dimly lit, steeped in the mingled scents of candle wax and old parchment. Matt's eyes adjusted to the glow spilling from an ornate chandelier overhead. Golden light flickered across wooden shelves, each stacked with worn books and scrolls, lining the walls in a rich tapestry of knowledge. For Matt, who'd spent most of his life in sunlit fields, this room must have felt like stepping into another world—a sanctuary of secrets and power.

Matt inhaled as if savoring the atmosphere. "The air here... it's different," he murmured. "Outside, I'm used to the smell of freshly tilled earth, the sharp tang of manure when the wind shifts, the wildflowers in bloom. But here... there's a richness. Something layered."

His hands, rough and calloused, tightened instinctively around the piece of firewood he'd brought for the hearth. He seemed to take quiet pleasure in the warmth radiating from the crackling flames. This warmth illuminated our faces but deepened the shadows beyond.

I looked at him, realizing just how much more there was to him. "You've lived a different life, Matt. You're not just another servant in this castle."

He lowered his head almost bashfully. "Thank you, My Prince. I owe much to you. You brought me into this castle and taught me to read and write. You showed me there's more to life than tilling fields and milking cows. For that, I'm forever grateful."

"In all those years working the land, did you ever wonder about life beyond our borders?"

He nodded. "Always. But the horizon was as far as my dreams could take me. Beyond that lay only kingdoms and lands I'd heard about in the stories you've read to me. Worlds that felt as unreachable as the stars. But you taught me something else: even distant dreams can be reached if one only dares."

I held his gaze, seeing in him a blend of humility and a pearl of newfound wisdom—a spirit grounded in the soil but reaching for the sky. "You mentioned those who leave and never come back. Do you think they found something better, something worth never returning for?"

"I can't say, My Prince. But I like to think there's another world out there where people like me could live free, not bound to the land they were born to. A place where we're limited only by our own will."

A smile tugged at the corner of my lips, the weight of his words settling within me. "Perhaps one day, Matt, we'll venture beyond this village, beyond these walls, and see the world as it truly is. And who knows? Maybe we'll find that place you speak of."

He smiled back, a glimmer of hope lighting his eyes like a lone star piercing the night. "I'd like that very much, My Prince. Very much indeed."

His voice softened. "What troubles you, My Prince?"

"Everything feels... uncanny as if I've been thrust into a story I didn't choose. A tale written by someone else. It's as though I've become a character, subject to the whims of an unknown author."

Matt regarded me thoughtfully, his brows furrowed as if unearthing a riddle. The candlelight flickered, casting dancing shadows that seemed to mimic our own tangled thoughts. The scent of aged books and melting wax filled the space. At the same time, beyond the heavy wooden door, the distant creak of floorboards and the howl of wolves in the moonlit forest heightened the sense of mystery. The room was warm, yet a chill had settled within me ever since I awoke here, as though I were no longer in control of my own fate.

He spoke softly. "I understand, My Prince. This castle is its own paradox—a place of wonders and horrors alike. It feels like these walls are alive, breathing with the centuries they've witnessed."

The weight of his words pressed against the strange certainty in my bones. Whatever fate awaited us, it was intertwined with the secrets held within this ancient fortress.

"TELL ME MORE ABOUT that night. What else happened? Anything that might help me remember?"

Matt hesitated, choosing his words carefully. "You were... quite disoriented when Günter brought you out of the moat. Your clothes were tattered, and your eyes were like pools of confusion. We led you to the Chamber of Reflections. That's where Count Corvin made his pronouncement."

"The Chamber of Reflections?" I echoed.

"Yes," Matt replied. "It's a room lined with mirrors—mirrors of all shapes and sizes. Some say those mirrors have mystical properties, that they reveal more than just your reflection. It was there that the Count declared your newfound status. He held an ancient, fragile scroll—stained and worn—claiming the fates themselves had decreed your arrival and role here."

"And you believe him?"

Matt looked uneasy, his gaze dropping to the floor before meeting mine again. "In this castle, My Prince, belief is... complex. We've all seen things and experienced phenomena that defy natural explanations. The Master is a man—or perhaps a being—of cryptic origins. To question him is to court danger."

"A man or a being, you say? So even his nature is ambiguous to you?"

"Exactly. There are whispers and rumors about his true form and powers. Some claim he can morph into animals, even elements. Others swear he's lived for centuries, recounting tales passed down through generations."

"Intriguing, yet perplexing," I said. "The enigma thickens."

"Indeed, My Prince. You are now part of this world—where every door could lead to another realm, where reality itself seems sculpted by those who dwell in the shadows."

I looked around, Matt's words settling over me like a cold fog on a cool morning. The room felt as if it were listening, breathing with us. The castle was not just my new home; it was a labyrinth of untold stories, each corner hiding a secret, each face concealing a tale. And I lost to my own past, which had now become the newest chapter in its age-old saga. It was both unsettling and oddly fitting—a paradox, just like the castle itself.

MY FIRST ENCOUNTER with Count Corvin was surreal, as though I'd stepped into a painting crafted by a mad artist, where every brushstroke carried layers of depth. His voice was a blend of silk and gravel as he welcomed me, filling the room with an intoxicating warmth. Just inhaling the air felt like drinking dark wine—full-bodied, rich, and infused with earthy undertones. The tapestries on the walls were woven with gold thread that shimmered like firelight, telling stories I somehow felt I'd always known but could never fully recall.

Then there was the tree in the library—a yew, ancient and imposing, with branches stretching to kiss alabaster and obsidian chandeliers. Candlelight flickered around it, casting shifting shadows that danced across its leaves and trunk. Every so often, the tree seemed to breathe, its bark pulsating as though it were alive, possessed by some otherworldly essence.

Count Corvin himself was fascinating. His eyes were like shards of sapphire, cool yet somehow warm, always reflecting a quiet, contemplative fire even when he laughed or discussed trivial matters. Those nights wandering through his dark, aromatic forests felt as though we were the only souls in existence. The scent of wet earth, the crunch of leaves underfoot, and the distant howl of an unseen animal created a symphony of isolation and intimacy. And when it rained, the castle transformed into an entirely different realm. In this place, the rhythmic drumming of droplets against stone echoed through hallways like haunting, ancient melodies.

We spoke of everything and nothing. Although the castle lacked the clutter of modern life, books filled every available space. Ancient scripts in indecipherable languages lay beside modern philosophical treatises. Sometimes, the Count would read passages aloud, his voice turning even the driest text into something profound, like a whispered secret. We discussed the elusive nature of time, the moral complexities of politics, and the paradoxes of religion. When he spoke of issues like the drug crisis, it was not with detachment but with the depth of someone who had witnessed the corrosive effects of addiction over centuries.

Yet, more than our conversations, more than the moonlit rides or feasts of unfamiliar delicacies, it was the indescribable comfort he provided, like a guardian I'd never known I needed. When he wasn't traveling to seek artifacts or meeting age-old acquaintances, he was there—sometimes across the hall, sometimes in the far reaches of his library. And even when miles separated us, it felt as though his presence lingered, woven into every nook and cranny of the castle.

During the day, he taught me the art of restfulness. The coffin, oddly enough, became a sanctuary—a silk-lined refuge from the questions swirling in my mind about my past. And the neck bites, strange as they might sound, became a ritual, an exchange of trust that felt as natural as breathing.

The Count was a mentor, a friend, and, in many ways, an enigma I never fully unraveled. But one thing was certain—our companionship, unconventional as it was, brought me a peace I had never known before.

THE AIR IN THE CHAMBER was cool and heavy with the mingled scents of lavender and parchment. Candlelight flickered against the stone walls, casting shadows that danced like restless spirits. The wood of the vanity was aged, its grain marked by years of silent witness to private confessions and long-buried secrets.

"Matt, do you think I'll ever remember who I truly am?" I asked, staring at my reflection in the ornate, brass-framed mirror. My face looked unfamiliar, as though it belonged to someone I once knew but had since forgotten.

Matt paused, his hands momentarily still as he folded a plush, emerald robe. "Would you want to remember?" he asked gently. "One of your books tells the story of a man who chose to forget, finding peace in ignorance. Perhaps you've found contentment in the life you have now."

I glanced at the shelves lining the room, filled with worn, leather-bound volumes, each one an invitation into worlds of ancient lore and complex human emotions. The faint rustle of a page-turning seemed to echo the unease within me. "You're wise, Matt," I said, the words escaping almost as a revelation. "Wiser than a servant ought to be."

"My Prince," Matt replied, nodding slightly, his gaze steady. "Shall I help you dress now?"

The urgency of the moment returned, the weight of obligations and unanswerable questions pressing down. "Is there enough time before the first bell rings?"

"You have time," Matt reassured, moving toward me with the robe in his hands, his presence a steady anchor in the drifting tides of my uncertainty.

Lost in the past for a moment, I found myself musing. "I remember when the Count first introduced you to me in this very chamber. You introduced yourself as my servant—a role I initially resisted, believing I could manage on my own."

Ah, the Count. Even now, I could almost hear the grating resonance of his voice filling the room, feel the sting of his temper sharp as acid. His reaction was swift and unforgiving, his fury a force that threatened to shake the very stones of the castle walls. Faced with his wrath, I chose to feign compliance. I suggested we pretend and keep our defiance hidden from his ever-watchful eyes.

But you, Matt, refused this clandestine approach. You embraced your role completely—dressing, undressing, feeding, even bathing me, as though your life depended on it. And in truth, it did. You had witnessed firsthand the merciless hand of Günter, the Count's enforcer, who dispensed death without hesitation to failed servants. Confronted with that fate, I learned to acclimate to having a servant, a concept that felt foreign to me in every way.

Now, standing in the same chamber, surrounded by the trappings of royalty and power, I found myself appreciating the care and attention that had become a strange, hidden strength—a quiet reminder that even princes are human.

Matt gently draped the robe over my shoulders, the fabric a soft, luxurious weight. Soon, the bell would ring from the castle tower, signaling the dawn of a new day and all the trials it would inevitably bring.

"Thank you, Matt," I murmured, meeting his gaze.

"Always at your service, my Prince," he replied, his voice infused with a devotion that surpassed the boundaries of mere duty.

So we continued, each playing our part in this grander story, the lines between master and servant, friend and confidant, blurring with each passing day. As I sat down, my robe shrouding me, the dimly lit chamber seemed to hold its breath, waiting as though the room itself recognized the gravity of our exchange.

I searched Matt's face for a sign of what he was thinking—a mixture of loyalty and something deeper, unspoken. Candlelight cast dancing shadows across the stone walls, painting an eerie, shifting pattern around us.

"Matt," I asked finally, "do you think I'll ever remember who I truly am?"

His hands paused briefly as he folded a plush emerald robe, his gaze steady on mine. "Would you want to remember?" he asked quietly. "One of your books tells the story of a man who chose to forget, finding peace in ignorance. Perhaps you're content with your present self and the past you have now."

His words lingered in the air, mingling with the faint scent of incense drifting from a nearby censer. Only the soft rustle of fabric and distant echoes of footsteps dared to break the silence that had fallen between us.

"You're wise beyond your station, Matt," I said, my voice softened with gratitude.

He gave a slight nod, a hint of pride in his expression. "Thank you, my Prince."

"Yes, Matt?"

"Shall I assist you in dressing now?" he asked, ever the diligent servant, his gaze both familiar and respectful.

I paused, memories flooding back to that first introduction when I had resisted the idea of a servant. The Count's reaction had been as swift as it was terrifying. Left with no choice, I pretended to accept it, even suggesting to Matt that we keep up the charade in secret. But he had refused, embracing his role with unwavering commitment, fully aware of what disobedience could mean under Günter's unyielding watch.

It was strange to think how far we'd come since then, how much I had come to appreciate his presence. "Is there enough time before the first bell rings?" I asked, feeling the weight of responsibilities I couldn't escape.

"There's time," Matt assured me. But even as he spoke, the bell's resonant clang echoed down the corridors, reverberating like a toll on lives shaped and bound by duty.

I stood barefoot on the cold stone floor, watching as Matt stirred the embers in the fireplace, the flames crackling in response. He returned with a carefully folded stack of garments, placing them atop my coffin with reverence. When our eyes met, an unspoken understanding passed between us. My own past was a maze of forgotten memories, but Matt's was etched in stone, woven with threads of loyalty and duty. Yet he bore it all without complaint.

He opened the first package, revealing boxers made from black silk. The fabric was cool and indulgent, wrapping around me with an almost conspiratorial intimacy. As Matt handed me the silk pants, their lightness and elegance became a testament to the life I was now living—both foreign and luxurious.

Matt grinned as he pulled on my socks, his fingers grazing the soles of my feet. "Ticklish today, are we?" His humor lightened the moment, and I chuckled, feeling a rare sense of ease. He slid on the Italian leather boots, each polished surface a mirror of its craftsmanship. Putting them on was like stepping into history itself, feeling the weight of hands long gone but whose legacy lived on.

As he applied gel to my hair, slicking it back into a ponytail, the scent of eucalyptus filled the air, cutting through the earthy aroma of woodsmoke and leather. "How do I look, Matt?"

He paused, taking in the ensemble. "You look dashing, my Prince," he said, his gaze heavy with something unspoken.

"Oh, the jewelry," I said, realizing the attire wasn't complete. I opened a velvet box to reveal platinum accents—a striking contrast to the dark fabric. Matt fastened the necklace around my neck, his earthy, familiar scent momentarily overwhelming me. His closeness was both a comfort and a reminder of what could never be.

When he placed the final pieces—the bracelet, the ring, the earrings, even the new piercing—I felt as though I were donning armor. The jewelry was beautiful, yes, but the adornment felt like both decoration and shield. Beneath it all, there were marks known only to us—the bruises on my neck, faint but present, a testament to my journey here.

"You're ready, my Prince," he whispered, his voice filled with quiet pride and something deeper, unguarded.

A tear escaped his eye, tracing a path down his cheek. I caught it with my thumb, tasting its salty testament to all we shared, to all the words left unsaid. "Don't cry," I whispered, pulling him close. I felt his body tremble as he returned the embrace and felt his tears warm against my chest. At that moment, I understood my role, not just as his prince but as his anchor and confidant.

As I held him, the chamber grew silent, a quiet sanctum bearing witness to the unspoken bond we'd forged. I realized then that beauty and sorrow often wore the same face, a face we both recognized intimately.

Drawing back just enough to see him clearly, I kept my arms around him, offering a brief sanctuary. "No matter where destiny takes us, Matt, remember what we've shared, what you've come to mean to me. You're so much more than this place ever intended."

His eyes widened as my words settled in. For a fleeting moment, I saw a glimpse of a different Matt, unbound by the walls of servitude, perhaps even dreaming of something more. His gaze drifted to the side as though he were holding on to this new self-image before it faded, committing it to memory, if only for a moment.

"BUT YOU MUSTN'T BE late for the Count," Matt finally said, stepping back and adjusting my cloak with a practiced, careful touch—a physical gesture that seemed to put emotional distance between us, as if to remind us of the boundaries we had to uphold in public. "He has great expectations for tonight, my Prince."

The word "Prince" lingered in the air between us, a title that felt both honoring and confining. I looked at him, my gaze tracing from his unruly hair to the shadows under his eyes, over the lines etched into his face by the twin forces of hardship and hope. No matter where destiny took me, this truth—this quiet connection we shared—was as much a part of me as the silk that clung to my body and the platinum that adorned my skin.

In a world determined to define us by our roles—master and servant, teacher and pupil—it reminded me that, in the end, we were simply two souls seeking solace in a place that offered so little. As the distant murmur of festivities grew louder, I knew this simple, irrevocable truth would be my most cherished armor for the night to come.

Matt's voice faltered slightly as he recited a line, his words hesitant, as if they bore a weight beyond mere ink and paper.

Outside, the scene unfolded in a lavish display. Carriages rolled up the gravel pathway like soft rainfall, each one a drifting vision from an opulent past, somehow blending with the mechanical marvels of the present. Through the slightly open window, a breeze carried the mingled fragrances of perfume, night-blooming jasmine, and the muskier scents of horse and leather. Every sight, sound, and scent felt like part of a meticulously orchestrated prelude to an extraordinary night.

I turned back to Matt, who lingered on the last syllable of his recitation. "Nevermore, that raven... u-uttered," he stammered softly, finding his voice again. "There's a certain gravity to that poem, isn't there?"

"A gravity that matches this night," I replied thoughtfully. "A night where worlds and eras seem to meet. Tell me, Matt—what else did you feel in those lines?"

Matt looked briefly at the coffin, then back at me. "A strange mix of dread and comfort. Like facing despair head-on might actually be the key to overcoming it."

"Well said," I replied, meeting his gaze. "Tonight is about facing many things: desire, despair, and the fleeting beauty that life—and even death—offers. But let's not dwell on the Raven's darkness tonight."

As if summoned by our words, the third bell began to toll, its sound deep and resonant, like the heartbeat of the castle itself, signaling that the awaited hour had arrived.

"My Prince," Matt said, his voice carrying a blend of excitement and trepidation, "Günter is at the door. It's time."

With a nod, I motioned for Matt to go ahead. He returned the cherished book carefully to its hiding place within the velvet-lined coffin, sealing it gently before stepping out. The somber weight of Poe's words lingered in the air, like an unfinished spell cast over the room, adding an air of mystery and foreboding.

Then, without warning, the door swung open, and Günter's imposing figure filled the threshold, his entrance as forceful as ever.

THE THIRD BELL TOLLED, its resonant chime echoing through the stone corridors—a summons that the evening's festivities were poised to begin. I moved to the window, where carriages gathered in the courtyard below, their polished surfaces gleaming under the night sky, each a glimmering vessel carrying guests who would soon fill the castle halls.

Behind me, I felt Matt's watchful gaze as he carefully placed the last book back in its hidden place within my coffin. For a brief moment, our eyes met—a silent exchange of unspoken words, a shared acknowledgment of the path before me. As he slipped from the room to prepare for the Count's arrival, I felt a pang of loss in the space he left behind.

Alone now, the memory of his touch lingered—a steadying hand, a grounding presence. Tonight, I would step into the unknown, adorned with titles and responsibilities that felt as heavy as they were grand, blessings and chains alike. Yet, in Matt's loyal gaze, I saw a reflection of my own silent dreams, those unspoken hopes that lay hidden beneath duty and expectation.

With one last glance out the window, I steeled myself, taking in the night's calm before the storm. The castle awaited, its walls alive with secrets and promises, and somewhere within, my place in its ancient story awaited, waiting to be written anew.

Dungeons

The moment Günter entered my cell, a chill prickled across my skin. Tonight, he appeared unsettlingly refined—an odd transformation from his usual grimy state. His sallow frame was polished to a sickly sheen, the bones of his arms and back seeming almost chiseled, while his hair, thin and limp, was slicked back into a meager ponytail. A trace of jasmine clung to him, hanging in the air like a malignant afterthought. Even his teeth were clean—a shocking departure from their usual state, littered with remnants of past meals. It was like meeting an entirely new monster clothed in familiar skin.

"Enjoying your time in the dungeon again, Günter?" I asked, my tone edged with disdain. "Or are you down here looking for faults in my servant and me to report back to the Count?"

He stepped forward into the dim circle of light that surrounded my chamber. A sneer curled across his lips.

"You're no different from the countless mortals who've passed through this castle," he spat. "You won't last with him long. You think you know him, but it's not you who has to endure his company when he's alone, despondent."

His words, sharp and slithering, sought to unsettle me. But I was prepared.

"Spare me the lecture, Günter. I'm well aware of the Count's tendencies. When he tires of a mortal, he'll discard me without a second thought. I'm not afraid of you. You're inconsequential to me."

I held his gaze, carefully choosing my next words. "Perhaps I should tell the Count about your... extracurricular activities in the dungeon. You know how much he despises your sadistic indulgences."

A flicker of uncertainty crossed his face, his disdain faltering for a moment. I felt a small surge of triumph.

"Don't be so hasty," he said, voice low and venomous. "You might learn sooner than you think just how 'inconsequential' I can be."

As he retreated, the scent of jasmine lingered in his wake. Günter was an enigma, and as long as I remained in Count Corvin's domain, I knew I'd have to solve the puzzle he posed or risk becoming another lost soul in this labyrinth of stone and sorrow.

"IT'S NOT AMUSEMENT," Günter growled suddenly. "Those fools and troublemakers need discipline."

"They're not all fools or troublemakers. They might just be innocents, caught in the wrong place at the wrong time," I countered, meeting his gaze unflinchingly.

"Is that what you think?" he scoffed. "I caught one of your 'innocents' just yesterday—a man lurking near the Count's chamber, trinkets jangling like a thief's alarm."

"Perhaps he's a traveler, a lost soul from a nearby town. You might consider releasing him."

Günter leaned against the cold stone wall, torchlight casting his gaunt face in shadowed relief. "He's locked away, secure in the dungeon. Resilience doesn't mean innocence. I'll make him talk, and he'll reveal what he's hiding."

"You're heading down there now, aren't you?" I said, unable to mask my contempt. "To torment him until he begs for mercy. Perhaps I'll inform the Count of your... approach to discipline."

I placed a steady hand on Matt's shoulder, who, as if on cue, grasped my waist and leaned in, tilting his neck provocatively as if inviting a bite—a silent signal, a reminder that we were players in a dangerous game.

Günter's sneer returned. "Your threats mean little to me," he said, cold and dismissive. "There are things darker than me lurking in this castle's shadows."

"Darker than you?" I mused, casting a quick glance at Matt. "Now that's a tale I'd love to hear. But we have other matters to attend to."

"Very well," he said, voice laced with bitterness. "But know this—I maintain order here, not to satisfy cruelty, but to preserve balance."

I locked eyes with him. "Then I'll be watching to ensure that's all you do."

Turning from him, Matt and I started down the hall, our footsteps echoing against the stone. Günter fancied himself a keeper of order, but his methods had become more than questionable. As his voice grated through the dim corridor, I felt its roughness as a tangible force.

"The Count awaits you at the main entrance to welcome the guests," he said, his words laced with condescension as he glanced at Matt. "And as for you, my dear 'biscuit,' you belong in the kitchen."

The faint scent of lavender mingled with the pungent odor of sweat and leather emanating from Günter, filling the hallway with a sour, unsettling aroma. His eyes swept over Matt, examining him as if he were an object rather than a person. I watched as Matt's expression shifted to vulnerability, instinctively stepping back toward the staircase. He knew those gloved hands would bring pain if I weren't here.

Countless nights, I'd dabbed antiseptic on Matt's bruises and cuts, relics of Günter's twisted diversions. I kept this knowledge hidden from Count Corvin, uncertain of the consequences if it came to light. Günter had always been too self-absorbed to realize I'd been tending to Matt's wounds.

I broke the silence. "Günter, make sure he's appropriately dressed for tonight."

Günter's eyes widened. "What?"

"You heard me," I said, voice clipped. "I never want to see Matt poorly dressed again."

With a begrudging nod, Günter spun on his heel, his coat tails flaring out as he exited, his scowl etched deep. The door clicked shut, and Matt exhaled, eyes full of gratitude. The oppressive atmosphere eased, and I knew we'd won a small victory in an ongoing war.

I turned back to Günter, my gaze unyielding. "Remember this, Günter. Lay a hand on Matt again, and I'll see to it that you end up in your own dungeon. You won't be the jailer—you'll be the prisoner."

The mildew-scented air seemed to thicken, mingling with the rusty odor of iron chains hanging from the walls. My eyes drifted to the "sweeper"—Günter's favored torture device lying menacingly in the corner.

"Should you hurt him again, I'll find a fitting punishment. You'll suffer in equal measure for every wound you've inflicted on him."

Günter's eyes flickered toward the device, and for a moment, true fear broke through his scowl.

"Try me, Günter. I'll make it my personal mission to turn your sadistic whims back on you. And don't think the Count's authority will protect you. If he finds out, I'll likely face execution—but for you, death will be neither swift nor merciful."

My fingers brushed the hilt of the dagger hidden beneath my cloak, letting the threat linger. "And if I must, I'll begin with your son. Imagine his face, twisted in agony, flesh seared by a heated iron—all in your name."

Günter blanched, fear breaking through his bravado.

"Make your choice wisely," I said, voice as cold as the stone surrounding us. "Cross me again, and you'll meet a storm you'll wish you'd never provoked."

Turning away, I left him trembling in the dark corridor. My steps echoed purposefully as I made my way to the ballroom. From behind, I heard him regain his composure, smoothing the fabric of his burgundy coat.

"My apologies for the earlier... disturbance," he muttered, tone guarded. He reached out, adjusting my cloak with a forced gentleness. "It grows colder as we go deeper into the castle."

He straightened my mask, positioning it just so, the gold and silver threads concealing enough of my face to maintain an air of mystery. For a fleeting moment, our eyes met.

"Shall we?" he asked, extending his arm. Formal yet unsettlingly close, I placed my hand on his forearm, feeling the stiff fabric beneath my fingers.

"Certainly," I replied.

Together, we descended the stone staircase. The air grew denser, thick with the scent of melted wax and ancient wood. From the ballroom, the murmur of conversation and the clink of glasses floated up, reminding me of the thin boundary separating us from the revelers above.

Günter led the way. "You wear intrigue well," he remarked, his tone oddly admiring.

"It's a masquerade ball," I replied. "The perfect place for it."

He chuckled softly. "Indeed. We're all playing our parts tonight."

I glanced down into the dark descent, apprehension settling over me. Casting a sidelong glance at Günter, I asked, "So, what awaits us below?"

He smirked. "Let's just call it... a revelatory experience."

Count Corvin

As I stepped onto the top stair, a line of gaslights flickered to life, casting their warm glow over the polished mahogany banister and the intricate runner that covered the staircase. Each light seemed to exhale with a life of its own, casting a soft, orange hue over the oil paintings lining the walls. The faint hum of burning gas filled the air, mingling with the distant strains of a violin warming up beyond my sight. It was as if I were descending through time, the ambiance evoking images of grand estates and whispered secrets under moonlit skies.

At the foot of the staircase, Count Corvin awaited me. He was the embodiment of Southern gallantry—at once timeless and somehow ageless. His attire was impeccable, a rich uniform of deep grays adorned with gold braiding and polished black boots. As I drew closer, I caught the mingling scents of aged bourbon and faint cigar smoke interlaced with fresh jasmine—a complex tapestry of aromas that perfectly complemented the man before me.

When I reached the bottom step, he looked up, our eyes meeting in the soft glow of the gaslight. His gaze held me, deep and enigmatic, and then his lips curved into a knowing smile.

"To my Phantom of the Opera," he murmured, his voice tinged with Northern aristocracy softened by Southern charm. "Would you join me in welcoming our illustrious guests this evening?"

"Of course, my General," I replied, my tone laced with reverence.

He extended his hand, and as I took it, I felt the strength of a man accustomed to command. His lips brushed mine briefly, and then, with a slight tilt of his head, he leaned closer, grazing my neck with his mouth. A shiver cascaded down my spine, a reminder of the wound that had never quite healed.

Turning us toward the grand archway that led to the main ballroom, he gestured gracefully. A canopy of jasmine blossoms framed the entrance as though nature itself was paying tribute to the splendor within.

"Welcome to the threshold of tonight's enchantments," he said softly. "Shall we?"

"Master, who are our guests tonight?" I asked, my gaze wandering over the towering, gold-leafed archways and ornate chandeliers. The hall was filled with an aromatic blend of sandalwood and vintage wines that made my head swim.

"Tonight, we are in remarkable company. First, we will greet the Gypsy Queen, a woman of wisdom and mystery, a seer of the unspoken. She leads the Major Arcana, each one possessing insight beyond mortal understanding."

"And the four houses of the Minor Arcana? What should I expect from them?"

The Count stepped closer, his cologne blending with the room's rich perfume. "They represent the elements: Cups for Water, Pentacles for Earth, Wands for Fire, and Swords for Air. They will present themselves, led by their Kings and Queens, followed by their Knights and Pages, each embodying their house's virtues."

"Are they here for me?" I asked, a nervous thrum quickening in my chest. His presence had always been my refuge, but stepping beyond that sanctuary felt unsettling.

"Yes, My Prince," he replied, his gaze meeting mine with an intensity that steadied me. "They come to speak with you, to stir the dormant fragments of your memory. Each of them holds a piece of your past."

"But my contentment lies here, in your company," I admitted, feeling the pull of an unknown future.

He placed a reassuring hand on my shoulder, warmth seeping into my bones. "I, too, find peace in your presence, but my soul is restless to uncover the intricate weavings of your forgotten history."

"Will it bring me pain?" I asked, uncertainty lacing my words.

"No," he said, cradling my face. "The memories will come as gifts, each presented by our guests tonight. They will unfold like a cascade, connecting you to the person you once were."

His words wrapped around me like a cloak, as if I stood on the edge of time itself, poised between the life I remembered and the life that awaited. As the first guests arrived, dressed in vibrant silks that glistened under the chandeliers, my heart surged with anticipation.

"As the night progresses, we shall engage in a tarot reading," Count Corvin said softly, his voice carrying an otherworldly resonance. The candlelight reflected in his eyes, casting golden flecks that seemed to peer into my soul.

"A tarot reading?" I repeated.

"A mystical game of divination," he explained, moving closer. "Through the arcana, we will reveal the tapestry of your past and, in doing so, craft a pathway to our shared future."

"But I am already committed to this present with you, Count. Why revisit what's already written?"

"Truth is my pursuit," he replied. "The past is not closed—it's a lens that sharpens our view of the present and illuminates the future. The unknown is our canvas, and we are the artists."

I exhaled slowly. "As you wish, Count Corvin. If this is the path you desire, then I shall follow."

His arms enveloped me in a gentle embrace, his fingers tracing a line before my eyes. "Close your eyes," he whispered. "Recall a single moment from this past year, one that shines brightest in your memory."

I let my eyelids fall, surrendering to his touch and the steady cadence of his voice. Memories flickered until one stood out vividly.

"We were in the courtyard under the harvest moon," I began. "You looked at me, really looked, and in that moment, I felt seen. You picked a night-blooming jasmine and tucked it behind my ear. The scent mingled with the cool night air, and for that moment, the world faded away."

When I opened my eyes, his gaze held mine, his smile soft yet unreadable.

"And so, it was written, and so it shall be," he murmured.

He took my hand, leading me toward the door that opened onto the courtyard. The soft creak of the door revealed a landscape drenched in moonlight, the moat stretching out before us in the dark, glassy calm. We walked, our steps muffled by thick foliage, the symphony of crickets creating a backdrop as natural as breathing.

Reaching the edge of the moat, the Count released my hand and sat on a stone bench. I joined him, both of us absorbing the scene in silence. The moon cast a silvery path across the water, shimmering like a bridge between worlds.

"It's beautiful," he whispered.

"Like a painting come to life," I replied. "There's a haunting tranquility here that I can't quite explain."

"Yes, much like the human heart—a mystery that beckons yet defies understanding." His gaze met mine, a probing look that seemed to search the depths of my soul. "What are you seeking, My Prince?"

"A connection," he answered, voice soft, "an echo that reaches across time. Can you feel it?"

I took a moment to consider. "There's a thread—a curiosity, a yearning for understanding—that defies explanation."

He nodded, his eyes never leaving mine. "Yearning often leads to enlightenment. Are you ready for the truths that await?"

"More than ready, Count," I replied, the hunger in my chest growing. "I feel a craving for understanding that only intensifies."

He smiled a deep, satisfied smile. "Then let this night be the canvas for that hunger, a tapestry woven from the threads of our souls."

We sat together in the shared silence, letting the night enveloped us. Finally, I broke the silence.

"Count, I find myself strangely content—as if part of me has come home. Yet, I wonder what tomorrow holds. Will the daylight erase this magic?"

He turned to me, his gaze warm and unyielding. "The sun may rise, and the world may change, but some things, My Prince, are eternal. What we uncover tonight will remain unchanged by dawn."

At that moment, all my fears dissolved, leaving only the truth that whatever lay ahead, this night, had connected us in ways that transcended time.

LATER, IN THE WARMTH of the castle, we shared a simple yet exquisite meal. I sat before a large bowl of Menudo, the aroma filling the room.

"You've honored tradition perfectly," I remarked, savoring each bite. "The Menudo tastes as if it were crafted with care."

"The culinary arts are to be revered, not transformed," he replied, his eyes gleaming. "In each spoonful, there is lime, cilantro, oregano—a taste that's both familiar and new, don't you think?"

"Yes, like alchemy. Every flavor melds together, an art in itself."

He nodded, watching me intently. "And this experience—does it connect you to the past?"

"Somewhat," I said, pausing. "It's like hearing a melody you can't place—familiar yet elusive."

"Just as you are to me," he murmured, stepping closer. Our eyes met, and for a moment, I felt as if I were looking into a mirror, reflecting back endless possibilities.

After our meal, he suggested moving to the drawing room, to which I eagerly agreed. Each room, each moment, felt like an unraveling—a deeper connection, a journey between souls.

As he led the way, the lingering scents, the soft lights, and the weight of shared silences left me feeling infinite.

The Gypsy Queen

Junior's eyes met mine as he swung open the door. They were a mesmerizing blend of emerald and gold, shifting with the room's low light. He nodded briefly, drawing my attention to the impeccable detail of his tuxedo, each stitch meticulously sewn, lending him an aura of timeless sophistication.

The air was rich with the scent of polished wood and the warm crackle of firewood from the grand fireplace in the hallway. Sandalwood and bergamot mingled with these aromas, emanating from Junior's cologne in a fragrance both grounding and alluring.

"Ladies and gentlemen," Junior announced, his voice filling the room with an almost musical cadence. "May I present to you the Gypsy Queen and the Major Arcana."

The grand chandelier above flickered, casting sporadic shadows across the walls. Conversations quieted, replaced by hushed anticipation, as a woman draped in crimson robes entered, her presence commanding the room. At her side was a man in a dark, decorated uniform adorned with gleaming medals. Their entrance seemed choreographed, each step measured as though heralding a series of yet-unseen wonders.

Junior stepped aside, bowing slightly as the Gypsy Queen passed, her smile mysterious beneath the sheer fabric of her headdress. Their eyes met in a brief, charged moment. Junior held the door, glancing behind her to ensure Major Arcana followed, then shut it with a practiced grace. Moving to a small table near the entrance, he picked up a golden bell and shook it lightly. Its clear, crystalline sound summoned waitstaff, who seemed to materialize from the shadows, circulating with trays of champagne and hors d'oeuvres.

For one so young, Junior moved through the space as if born to it—a prince in a kingdom of opulence and intrigue. He was a luminous presence amid the evening's enigma, an anchor within the tapestry of splendor woven by his lineage. Tonight, he was at the center of the unfolding drama, a silent yet powerful force that none could ignore.

As guests whispered and mingled, I felt myself captivated not only by the spectacle of the evening but by Junior himself. In him was a grace and gravitas that set him apart, and as I looked around, I realized I wasn't alone in my fascination.

The night's allure deepened when the Gypsy Queen, Arcana, entered fully, her formidable presence expanding to fill the space. She was clothed in fitted black leather, her form exuding a potent combination of power and sensuality. Her fiery red curls cascaded over her shoulders, catching the light as they moved. Her eyes, dark and intense, seemed to see into the souls around her while her lips, a shade as rich as midnight roses, hinted at secrets. Her porcelain skin formed a striking contrast to her dark attire, amplifying her magnetic allure.

A complex blend of incense and exotic spices drifted through the room as she walked, leaving a faint, arcane aroma in her wake. Her footsteps were a soft rhythm, a symphony in cadence that commanded attention with subtle authority.

"Count Corvin," she said, her voice a smoky blend of mystery and amusement, "it's a pleasure to attend your gathering. My abode and I eagerly anticipate tonight's festivities."

"Arcana," Count Corvin replied, his voice resonant with cultured warmth. "It's always a pleasure to see you."

Their eyes met in an unspoken dialogue, a silent exchange layered with understanding. Then Arcana turned her gaze toward me, each step deliberate as she approached, her hand extended.

"Is this your new companion?" she asked, her tone both welcoming and inquisitive.

"Hello, Your Majesty. Welcome to the party," I said, stammering slightly under the weight of her gaze. I took her hand, pressing my lips lightly against it. Her skin was cool, almost startling against the warmth of mine.

"Allow me to see your right hand," she said, her tone a delicate blend of invitation and command. Intrigued, I offered my hand.

"Call me Arcana," she said, a faint smile diffusing the intensity of the moment.

Her fingers traced the lines of my palm with gentle precision, her voice weaving a narrative as she read my hand.

"Your heart line," she began, "tells of an inner world shaped as much by your internal dialogues as by the world outside. You are a universe unto yourself, unbound by expectations or conventions. Remember, you alone hold the pen to your destiny. Life is an unwritten poem, awaiting your verses."

A lump formed in my throat as her words resonated deeply. "Thank you, Arcana," I managed, my voice thick with emotion.

She withdrew her hand, her gaze piercing as though she were searching my soul for secrets.

"My Prince, you are as yet unnamed, but names alone do not define identity. Each of us here will offer you a gift tonight, something to stir up your lost memories. My gift is unique: an understanding of the source of your affliction. It is a hidden illness, felt more than seen. Tonight, you will have the chance to confront it."

Her words sent a chill down my spine, and as I held her gaze, I felt the first stirrings of a journey—a path that would lead to revelation and confrontation.

I SAT AT THE WORN OAK table, the knots in the wood as familiar to me as my own skin. Manuel was beside me, his playful dimples belying a sharper insight than most people gave him credit for. We looked alike in our shared dark hair and eyes, inherited from our father, yet our personalities were worlds apart.

To my left, my mother, Rosa, glanced nervously toward my father, Juan, who leaned against the doorframe, a glass of liquor in hand, his face unreadable.

"The children should be in school, Juan. Now isn't the time for rash decisions," Rosa said, her voice laced with worry.

Tia Maria intervened, her voice weathered with wisdom. "Rosa, life often brings storms we cannot control. All we can do is find a safe harbor and wait until they pass."

She sipped her coffee, her gaze meeting mine as she set the cup down.

"As for you two," she said, looking at Manuel and me, "school will teach you many things, but it can't teach you how to be a family."

Father stepped into the room, placing his glass on a side table with a soft clink. "Maria's right. We need to be together, especially now."

Manuel broke the silence. "Are we going to live here now?"

Tia Maria chuckled, her laughter softening the tension. "Not quite, Mijo. But for now, this is home."

The kitchen timer sounded—a sharp, jarring contrast to the low murmur of our conversation. Tia Maria rose, her movements defying her age. As she opened the oven, the warm aroma of tamales filled the room. It felt as though the walls expanded, embracing us in a cocoon woven from the threads of love and resilience.

As I bit into the tamale she placed before me, its flavors vibrant and comforting, I felt as though I were consuming a piece of our family's strength—a strength forged through hardship yet enduring.

COUNT CORVIN'S VOICE brought me back to the present, a calm anchor amidst the swirling memories.

"Good lad, do not be timid," he assured me, his tone gentle yet commanding. "My home is a sanctuary for you tonight. The residents are eager to meet you."

Arcana inclined her head in a graceful bow. "Until we meet again," she whispered, then took the arm of an attendant dressed in gold embroidery, gliding toward the grand ballroom.

I watched as a procession of guests followed, each clad in intricate attire, each a mystery in their own right. Perfumes and colognes thickened the air with notes of musk, lavender, and spices, adding layers to the atmosphere. Their whispered conversations wove together like a tapestry of riddles and unfinished thoughts.

Among them was a jester, his costume a riot of colors accented with bells that jingled softly. A figure beside him was garbed as a celestial star, crystals embedded in the fabric shimmering with each step. Others wore a crown of golden rays, representing the sun. In contrast, others wore religious vestments and garments from myth and legend. Each costume seemed a story waiting to be told, a living page from an unwritten book.

"It's a spectacle, isn't it?" Count Corvin murmured at my side, his gaze sweeping over the scene. "Each costume, each face, a story yet to be revealed."

Before I could respond, the chime of a bell filled the mansion, its sound resonant and lingering. Three chimes in total, marking the night's beginning.

"The evening has officially begun," the Count said, his voice solemn. "Prepare yourself for an unforgettable journey."

As I stood beside him, steady in his presence, I wondered what roles we would play tonight—and what stories awaited their telling in the hours yet to come.

Prometheus

The atmosphere in the room shifted the moment Junior approached the ornate wooden door. His movements were as measured as ever, each step calculated—until he stumbled over an irregular stone in the floor, causing a murmur to ripple through the crowd. Junior recovered quickly, meeting my gaze briefly with a look of faint embarrassment. Composed once more, he reached for the handle, a masterpiece of silver and emerald, and swung the door open.

"Allow me to introduce Prometheus, Titan, son of Iapetus and Themis," Junior announced, his voice regaining its musical cadence.

Prometheus entered, towering and formidable. He exuded both power and elegance, holding an elemental staff adorned with small branches that glowed with a subtle inner light. His hair, black with streaks of silver, flowed to his shoulders. His piercing, intelligent eyes scanned the room, taking in every detail with intensity.

He wore a tunic of a color that seemed caught between dusk and dawn, covering one shoulder and flowing down to his knees. A golden rope, intricately woven to resemble intertwined serpents, held the fabric together, bestowing upon him an aura of both majesty and danger. His sandals left faint, smoldering marks on the marble floor with each step, as though fire and brimstone walked with him.

The scent he brought with him was equally striking—a mix of smoky oak, fresh sage, and the sharp tang of flint, giving the impression that he had emerged from a place both ancient and elemental.

"My Lord," Prometheus intoned, his voice rich and warm yet carrying an unmistakable edge of authority, "thank you for inviting me to this occasion. Your thoughtfulness does not go unnoticed."

Count Corvin bowed deeply. "Thank you, Prometheus, for bestowing life and fire upon us. My debt to you is immeasurable."

Prometheus's gaze lingered on the Count, his expression a blend of acknowledgment and gentle reproach. "Bestowing fire was both my gift and my burden, Count. Debt is a human concept, and such constructs hold no power over divine actions. Still, I am pleased to witness the embers of my legacy burning within your civilization."

The air felt charged, as though the boundary between mortal and divine had thinned. Then, Prometheus turned to me, his gaze filled with an otherworldly light.

"My son," he began, "I bring you a gift to aid you tonight." From his hand, he extended a hollowed branch with faintly smoldering coals nestled within. The scent of burnt cedar filled the air as he held it out to me.

"This branch," he continued, "contains coals from the realm of the gods. With it comes energy, willpower, desire, and charisma. The House of Wands will guide you through your past and future. Tonight will be a remarkable learning experience."

I was silent for a moment, awestruck by the intensity of his presence and the magnitude of his gift. Finally, I extended my hand, fingers brushing the branch, and felt a warm pulse of energy surge through me as though the coals were whispering ancient secrets directly into my veins.

"Thank you, sir," I managed, my voice barely a whisper.

As I examined the branch, I noticed new sprigs beginning to unfurl, tiny leaves filled with vitality. Before I could take it all in, the twigs detached themselves, drifting down in delicate spirals, vanishing in a shower of sparkling light before they touched the ground.

Prometheus chuckled softly. "Even the smallest offshoots of this branch hold the fire of transformation. Use it wisely to uncover your past and to forge the narrative of your future."

The weight of his words settled upon me. Tonight was not just another night; it was a turning point. I tightened my grip on the branch, feeling its warmth seep into my skin.

"I will, sir. I won't let this gift—or this night—go to waste."

Prometheus inclined his head. "Then go forth, my son. Illuminate the path ahead, and let the House of Wands guide you through the maze of your existence."

With the branch glowing softly in my grasp, I felt a newfound clarity, an eagerness to embrace whatever lay ahead.

OUTSIDE THE CONVENTION center, the sounds of clinking glasses and murmured congratulations faded into the background as Collin and I found a quiet spot. The cool evening breeze tousled my hair and brought a welcome calm.

"I appreciate you coming to my graduation," I said, fidgeting with the tassel on my robe.

"Of course," Collin replied, his voice as warm as his familiar smile. He wore his favorite blue pinstriped shirt and khakis, his potbelly a testament to his years spent savoring life. He reached out for a hug, and I playfully nudged him away.

Three years of friendship and something more hung in the air between us, a mix of connection and indecision that neither of us had fully acknowledged.

"You know, we could be more if you'd just make up your mind," he teased, his dry humor softening the moment.

I sighed, looking away. "I know, but my family's opinion matters. It's not just disapproval—they can be harsh."

"Family is complicated," he murmured, his understanding clear.

"Yeah, it is."

"Is your family doing anything special for you tonight?" he asked.

"My father's hosting a barbecue," I replied. "Friends will be there."

"Am I included in that list?"

I hesitated, then shook my head. "Not yet, Collin. I'm sorry."

He chuckled softly. "I get it. By the way, you look great in that robe." He reached over to adjust the tassel, his fingers light.

Elaine appeared, breathless, scanning the crowd before spotting us. "Aaron, your mom's looking for you," she called, slipping her arm through mine.

Collin watched us with a faint smile. "Guess I'll head off. Enjoy your party," he said, giving me a quick hug before walking away. As he disappeared into the crowd, the ambiguity of our relationship stretched out like a shadow. I let Elaine pull me back toward family and celebration, but a small part of me lingered with him, unresolved.

THE PARTY'S LAUGHTER and chatter filled the air. String lights illuminated the backyard, casting a soft glow on guests who milled about with drinks in hand. A playlist of indie and classic rock floated through the speakers, curated by my brother Manuel.

As I made my way through the crowd, Sierra waved me over and handed me a small gift. I unwrapped it to reveal a beautiful porcelain brooch. "It's unique," I murmured, touched by the thoughtfulness.

My father was tending the barbecue, a picture of concentration as he flipped burgers and sipped his beer. We hadn't spoken since the ceremony, and his silence loomed.

"Is that guy your boyfriend?" Elaine asked, nodding in the direction Collin had taken. I hesitated, feeling a swirl of emotions.

"Maybe," I replied, still uncertain.

Elaine shrugged, accepting my answer. "It's your life. Besides, today's all about you and finally earning your degree."

"Yeah," I said, my gaze drifting to my father, who had just handed the grilling duties to Manuel.

"I just wish I could read him," I admitted.

"Parents are complicated," Elaine said. "He's probably just processing everything in his own way."

I nodded, giving her a grateful smile. "You're right. Thanks for being here."

She patted my arm. "Go enjoy the rest of your day. This is your time."

I moved through the guests, stopping to talk, share laughs, and thank friends and family. The air was filled with the smell of barbecue mingling with the earthy scent from the rabbit corral, a strangely grounding aroma in the whirlwind of celebration.

***

AS THE NIGHT DEEPENED, my father grew more unsteady, his movements looser as he downed another glass of whiskey. Suddenly, he clapped his hands, capturing everyone's attention.

"Tonight, we celebrate my son!" he announced, pressing play on an old tape deck. A lively Spanish tune filled the air, its melody laced with nostalgia.

To my surprise, my father began to sing, his voice unexpectedly tender, harmonizing with the music. This rare display of affection, whether genuine or laced with irony, left me confused. The crowd applauded as he finished, lifting their glasses in toasts.

Despite the warmth of the celebration, I felt a pang of uncertainty. Tonight, I realized that it was not just about my achievements but also a confrontation with the unresolved—my relationship with my father, my connection with Collin, and the life I was just beginning to shape.

THE CHIMING OF THE bell over the ballroom's entrance signaled another arrival. The grand double doors opened slowly, revealing Prometheus, who entered with an air of effortless command. His dark velvet suit caught the chandelier's glow, each step accompanied by an entourage clad in equally rich attire.

The room fell silent as Prometheus approached me, his eyes glinting with amusement. "Good evening, Prometheus. Your arrival is as dramatic as ever," I greeted him, extending my hand.

"Dramatic entrances are half the fun, don't you think?" he replied, his voice smooth as silk. I gestured to his entourage.

"And who are your companions tonight?"

"They are friends, associates, and some might even say protectors," he said with a knowing smile. He nodded toward his entourage, who offered polite acknowledgments in return.

"Protectors?" I raised an eyebrow. "Is there something I should be worried about?"

Prometheus chuckled softly. "Concerned? No. But
a little extra protection never hurts in a world as unpredictable as ours."

"Very well," I said, gesturing to the main table. "Make yourselves comfortable. The night has only begun."

As Prometheus and his entourage took their seats, the rest of the guests resumed their conversations, but the atmosphere had shifted. His presence had changed the energy of the room, adding an air of mystery that left me both intrigued and slightly wary.

As I continued my duties as host, I felt Prometheus's gaze follow me. Each word he spoke, each gesture he made, felt like pieces of a puzzle I was only beginning to understand. Tonight promised more than celebration—it promised revelation.

Mary Magdalen

Junior cleared his throat, his voice amplified with a dignified resonance.

"Ladies and gentlemen," he began, his gaze sweeping across the room. "It is my honor to present a woman of unparalleled significance—a divine mystery made flesh—Mary Magdalene, wife of Jesus of Nazareth."

As his words faded, Mary Magdalene entered. The atmosphere seemed to shift around her, quieting as if the air itself recognized her presence. Her eyes held a depth of ancient wisdom, their gaze calm and all-encompassing. Her skin, kissed by the Mediterranean sun, seemed to emit a natural glow, contrasting vividly with her raven-dark hair beneath a pristine white veil. She moved forward, each step graceful, as though she hovered between two realms—the ethereal and the real. Her scarlet robe draped around her like a river, regal yet humble, bold yet subdued.

In her hands, she held a golden chalice. On closer inspection, I saw that it shimmered with intricate filigree—a weave of interlocking patterns that evoked the solemn beauty of scripture. The object was rich with history, a testament of faith and sacrifice.

"Thank you, Junior, for your introduction," she said, her voice gentle yet charged with authority.

Mary Magdalene addressed the room with serene composure, "And thank you all for your presence here. We gather tonight to unearth truths and to dismantle illusions. This evening, we convene in the spirit of divine union and revelation."

Her words reverberated with a power that seemed to linger in the air, almost tangible as it settled around us. She turned to Count Corvin, her voice lowering into a private, practically affectionate tone.

"Count Corvin," she said, "your gracious invitation is deeply appreciated. The memory of our last meeting still lingers in the air of France."

Count Corvin moved forward, taking her extended hand—adorned with rings that gleamed aquamarine and lapis lazuli—and pressed his lips to it in a gesture of deep respect.

Then she turned to me, a soft smile lifting the corners of her mouth. "So, this is the young prince I've heard of." Her eyes sparkled, and warmth radiated from her touch as her hand reached toward mine. "Young Prince," she said, her voice soft but intent, "I hear you follow the Catholic faith. Has your spiritual journey borne fruit?"

Mary Magdalene's words resonated within me, but before I could answer, she moved toward a table adorned with sacred relics, scriptures, and ornate candleholders. From it, she lifted a golden chalice, its engraved patterns narrating the story of crucifixion and resurrection. Filled with a deep red wine that glinted in the candlelight, it was a vessel both sacred and powerful.

"This chalice holds the essence of my husband, Jesus Christ, our Savior," she said, offering it to me. "Accept it as a token of my esteem."

The room grew still, charged with a reverence that seemed to weigh on every breath. Around Mary Magdalene, symbols of Cups adorned the space, reflecting the emotional and spiritual dominion she held—the elements of the moon, of dreams, and of the hidden mysteries of the soul.

With a humbled heart, I replied, "I accept this with gratitude."

As I took the chalice from her hands, her fingers brushed my cheek in a gesture that slowed time. Each second stretched, allowing me to absorb the full weight of her blessing. Centuries of wisdom and the delicate power of divine love flowed through that touch.

She leaned in close, her voice a whisper only I could hear. "May this night bestow upon you revelations that words could scarcely contain."

"PAXIL IS OFTEN PRESCRIBED for depression and anxiety, but it's not a universal solution," the doctor explained, his voice calm but certain.

"Exactly, Doctor," I replied. "That's why I've been hesitant."

The room fell silent, filled only by the soft hum of his computer. He glanced down to jot notes, his expression thoughtful, his years of experience showing in the lines etched across his forehead.

"In your military service, did you experience any particularly traumatic events?" he asked, his tone shifting to something gentler.

I hesitated. "I wasn't on the front lines, but the danger was ever-present. One night, a mortar fire hit our base. Shrapnel tore through the tents. The sounds, the screams—they stayed with me. You don't forget that."

He met my gaze, his eyes reflecting a deep understanding. "Experiences like that leave scars that armor can't protect against."

I nodded, feeling the weight of those memories settle between us.

"As we move forward, understand that your military experience will play an essential role in therapy. Have you attended counseling before?"

"Just the mandatory sessions during service," I admitted. "They were more procedural than therapeutic."

"All too common, I'm afraid," he sighed, scribbling another note. "What troubles you most right now?"

"Everything feels like a fog," I confessed. "Even simple things like my nephews' laughter sound harsh, almost unbearable."

He put down his pen and leaned back. "I can't promise quick fixes, Mr. Fragoso. But clarity is attainable, and you're not alone on this path."

"CAN YOU SHARE ANY OTHER experiences that felt out of the ordinary, things you thought weren't typical?" he asked.

I fidgeted with the hem of my shirt, struggling for words. "Well... I once walked out of work in the middle of the day. No two-week notice, not even a sick excuse."

He encouraged me to continue, his pen poised.

"I drove straight to my mom's place, thinking maybe she'd understand, but when I arrived, she was busy setting up for a charity event. She barely looked up. 'We'll talk later, sweetie,' she said. So, I left."

"Did you go back to your apartment?"

"Yes, but then I had a ridiculous argument with my roommate over leftover pizza. It was like I was caged, pacing. I looked at my car keys, and the next thing I knew, I was driving to Santa Cruz."

"Santa Cruz? From Las Vegas?"

"Yeah, it didn't make any sense. But I rolled down the windows, let the wind drown everything out, and the smell of the ocean hit me as I got closer. It felt like freedom."

"Did you visit anyone there?"

"I stayed with a friend. Crashed on her couch for a week. I found a temp job at a beach café just to get by. Then, reality hit—I got a call from a coworker reminding me of my job. So, I drove back."

Dr. Mitchell listened, a frown forming. "Depression alone wouldn't account for this behavior," he said, putting down his pen thoughtfully.

"But I was diagnosed with depression years ago," I protested.

He nodded. "Mental health diagnosis evolves over time. Your symptoms align more with Bipolar Disorder."

"Bipolar?" I repeated, the word feeling foreign yet strangely fitting.

"Yes. This accounts for the impulsive trip and the fluctuations in mood. Bipolar disorder often presents as depression initially, but its cycles of highs and lows paint a different picture."

I looked down, my hands shaking. "So, what now?"

Dr. Mitchell moved closer, offering a reassuring smile. "Take a breath. We have treatments, medications, and support. You'll manage this—I promise."

As I left his office, the scent of lavender lingered in my nostrils, and the new diagnosis rang in my mind. Bipolar Disorder—a word that reshaped my understanding of myself, each piece of my past suddenly fitting into place.

In the silent air outside, I breathed in deeply. Perhaps, at last, I had found the lens through which I could bring my life into focus.

Ashikaga Takauji

"Count," Junior announced, his voice carrying a sense of reverence and excitement. "I have the distinct honor of introducing Ashikaga Takauji, the legendary samurai and shogun of Japan."

The Count's attention turned toward Takauji, who entered the room with a low, dignified bow. His dark, lacquered armor caught the light, its intricate details casting shadows that seemed to breathe.

"Greetings, my Lord," Takauji said in a calm, measured voice, the rich timbre of his words carrying the weight of centuries. "I am grateful for your invitation. It is an honor to be here on your esteemed soil."

"Your presence graces us all, Mr. Takauji. My last sojourn to Japan was enlightening, a vivid tapestry of tradition and progress. Tell me, how fares your land now?"

Takauji straightened, his gaze steady. "Japan thrives. It is a nation woven from the fibers of the ancient and the modern, each thread a testament to its resilience and grace."

"An admirable paradox," the Count replied thoughtfully.

Takauji's eyes met mine as he approached, the light from the chandelier casting glints across the intricate cherry blossom and dragon etchings on his armor—symbols that nodded to his heritage as both warrior and leader. A subtle scent of sandalwood drifted from his robes, grounding him in tradition while accentuating the quiet power he radiated.

"You must be the new Prince," he observed, his voice carrying an authority that felt almost sacred.

"Yes, Mr. Takauji." I bowed deeply, my heart pounding as I felt the Count's approving gaze on me.

Takauji inclined his head, lifting his arm in a graceful gesture. "In my time, I led soldiers, upheld justice, and served as a Shogun among the Ashikaga, yet I was equally deemed a traitor and a villain in my country's history."

His voice held a quiet gravity as he spoke, and I could see the shadows of the past flicker across his eyes—a soldier, a leader, yet a man marked by contradictions.

"For this occasion," he continued, "I bring a gift." With a subtle nod, one of his guards approached, carrying a beautifully crafted wooden box. Takauji opened it with the care of one, unveiling a relic. Inside, nestled in velvet, was a sword of ethereal beauty, its polished blade catching the light with a cold gleam.

"This sword embodies the essence of air," he explained, his eyes intent. "It symbolizes truth and the dual nature of judgment, for the blade cuts both ways. Use it wisely, and let it remind you that the judgments we pass upon others reflect back upon us."

Awed, I reached out, my fingers brushing the hilt. The weight was steady and grounding, the cold steel a silent reminder of its history and its power. Takauji's gaze was unyielding as he watched me lift the sword from its resting place.

Finally, with a measured nod, he turned to his escort, a silent signal that it was time to depart. The Count and I watched him as he retreated into the shadows, his quiet strength lingering in the room long after he had gone.

THE SIMMERING ANGER that had seized me earlier began to dissipate as I stood by Dori's car, her calm presence a balm against the storm inside me.

"Fine, let's go," I said, giving in, though my pride made it difficult to admit she was right.

Dori unlocked her car—a sleek convertible that suited her vibrant, free-spirited charm. The jingle of her keys felt oddly soothing, as if part of a private symphony just for her.

Sliding into the passenger seat, I breathed in the new car smell mingling with her soft, floral perfume. It was grounding, making the confined space feel oddly intimate. She turned the key, and the engine purred to life, its gentle hum offering a counterbalance to the remnants of my frustration.

"You mentioned a charming bar?" I asked, breaking the silence.

"Yeah, it's called The Velvet Moon. It's quirky but has a certain magic to it. You might like it."

"The Velvet Moon?" I raised an eyebrow. "Sounds like the kind of place a werewolf would hang out."

She laughed, a sound so warm it melted the last of my lingering irritation. "Well, it's not a full moon tonight, so I think we're safe."

As she maneuvered the car along winding roads, her calm skill at the wheel began to work its own kind of therapy on me. It was hard to hold onto anger with Dori's quiet serenity by my side.

"Aaron, family can be overwhelming. Sometimes we say things we don't mean just to lash out," she said gently, her eyes focused on the road.

"Yeah, well, this time I meant it," I muttered. "Santino acts like he owns me, like he's the boss of my life just because he's older."

Dori pulled into the parking lot of The Velvet Moon. The building was an old relic, its neon lights flickering above the entrance, casting a soft glow over the cobblestone path leading inside.

"Let's talk it out over a drink," she said, killing the engine. Her sideways glance held warmth and something like understanding.

I nodded, stepping out of the car. Sometimes, I thought that escape didn't mean running away. It could mean creating space to confront what you'd been avoiding—especially if that meant facing yourself.

⚜

SEATED ACROSS FROM Dori at the bar, the weight of her gaze made me shift slightly.

"I manage with therapy, medication, and a strong support system," she said, putting out her cigarette. "You could use the same."

The jasmine scent from her perfume mixed with the smoky air, enveloping me. She leaned in, her eyes piercing. "These issues won't resolve on their own, Aaron. Sometimes, you have to let someone in."

My gaze flicked to the bartender, who caught my eye and gave me a friendly wink. I looked away, feeling a bit sheepish under Dori's watchful stare.

"I can't just pretend my emotional mess will sort itself out," I said, my voice low. "And dating a bartender isn't the solution."

"Maybe not," she replied. "But letting someone into your life might be a start. You can't keep bottling everything up."

Just then, my favorite '80s tune played over the speakers, and I felt my mood lighten as I let the music wash over me. It had been ages since I allowed myself to feel this relaxed, and Dori noticed, smiling knowingly.

"You love this song," she said, tapping her glass. "It's a reminder that the real you is still in there. Maybe that's where you'll find the answers you're looking for."

I pondered her words, taking a sip of my White Russian. The mix of vodka and coffee liqueur, with just the right amount of cream, felt like comfort itself.

"Maybe you're right," I said. "Maybe I need to start searching for that version of me."

Dori lifted her glass for a toast. "First step—ask that bartender for his number."

Laughing, I shook my head. "Alright, let's not get too ahead of ourselves. But I'll consider it."

We clinked glasses, the thumping '80s beat filling the air around us. For the first time in a long while, I felt a strange but welcome optimism. I didn't have all the answers, but I was finally asking the right questions.

The night went on, the music shifted to a softer ballad, and the room seemed to echo the bittersweet nature of our conversation. Dori tossed back another shot, her eyes sharp as she turned to me.

"You're more than just a caretaker, Aaron. There's a whole person in there who deserves to be seen."

I nodded, looking down at my shot glass. "But how do I even begin?"

"Start small," she said simply. "Do something for yourself. Even if it's just asking someone out."

Taking her advice to heart, I glanced back at the bartender, who caught my look with a playful smile. With a deep breath, I slid my phone across the bar. He took it, typing his number with a grin.

As he walked away, I felt a faint brush of warmth—a small but meaningful leap off the tightrope I'd been walking for so long. Dori laughed, pleased with herself.

"See? Not so bad."

I grinned, savoring the moment. This wasn't just about the bartender; it was about reclaiming pieces of myself, about taking the first tentative steps onto solid ground.

AS MR. TAKAUJI PREPARED to leave, he turned to me one last time, his gaze intense.

"May this sword guide you on your journey to leadership and self-discovery," he said, bowing deeply.

Guided by his escort, he moved toward the ballroom, the soft rustle of his robes and the clink of his armor punctuating his departure. Each of his men clutched their own swords, their movements like a quiet, reverent symphony.

As they disappeared into the shadows, I looked down at the sword in my hands. Its weight felt grounding, as if anchoring me to something deeper, more resolute. The air seemed to shift in their wake, leaving behind a lingering sense of purpose.

Hermes

Junior's voice echoed through the hall, each word carrying a weight that settled heavily over the crowd.

"Presenting Hermes, Messenger of the Gods, Son of Zeus and Maia."

All eyes turned as Hermes entered, a figure exuding an energy that was both grounded and otherworldly. He was tall, yes, but it wasn't just his height that held attention—it was the way he seemed to hover between the mortal and the divine. His short brown hair framed a face marked by the mischievous wit of an immortal, and from his helmet and sandals, small wings vibrated softly as if holding back a storm.

In his hand, he carried a staff adorned with two entwined serpents, their eyes tiny gemstones that glinted with an internal light. He also held a large golden coin, a symbol of transactions that moved between gods and mortals. He stopped in front of the Count and bowed with a fluid grace that felt like watching light bending through the water.

"I stand before you as Hermes," he announced, his voice deep and resonant, "emissary to the mortal realms and messenger of the divine. How may I serve on this auspicious night?"

The Count cleared his throat, meeting Hermes's gaze steadily.

"Your presence truly elevates the occasion, Hermes. Do enlighten us—what brings you to this realm tonight?"

Hermes smiled, his eyes twinkling with an intensity that felt electric.

"The winds of change are blowing, Count. They whisper of untold destinies, of cosmic scales tipping in favor of monumental events. Your role, I think, is yet to be revealed."

At his words, the room seemed to constrict, every guest holding their breath. Hermes turned and took a step into the Count's residence, his gaze moving to the Count.

"Van, it's delightful of you to extend an invitation here in this new land. I'm eager to see what amusement you've prepared for us this evening."

"You never fail to bring your playful spirit, Hermes," the Count replied, his voice warm. "How fares your father?"

A sly smile crossed Hermes's face. "He fares well, as always, casting thunderbolts here and there in his usual, rather dramatic way. He sends his regards."

As Hermes continued, his iridescent eyes shifted to me with a sudden intensity.

"You must be the new Prince," he remarked, his voice thoughtful. "Platinum graces you elegantly, yet gold and fortune call to you."

With that, Hermes extended a hand, and from thin air, he produced a gleaming gold coin embossed with a five-pointed star. As he held it out, the coin twisted and turned in the dim light as if alive. I reached out, and as our fingers brushed, a wave of warmth spiraled up my arm.

"My domain embodies the material realm," he said, his voice like the gentle chime of coins. "I am the god of alchemy and trade, of wealth and exchange—though I am also the patron of thieves. Quite the paradox, wouldn't you agree?"

"So, what does this mean for me?" I asked, trying to ignore the coin's surprising weight in my hand.

He chuckled, a sound as rich as gold itself. "Tonight, you'll explore where you place your value. Understand the ebb and flow of what you hold dear, and remember: never jeopardize your kin for wealth."

I PLACED MY PHONE FACE down, its screen fading to darkness as my thoughts spiraled. Dean's voice had been laced with that familiar condescension, the subtle cruelty masquerading as concern. In another reality, he might have been genuinely worried, but here, his words were barbed, laced with reminders of my past mistakes.

I glanced at my laptop, its idle screensaver flickering like a restless firefly. It was irresponsible to leave it on, I knew, but I wasn't exactly vying for "Roommate of the Year." My gaze shifted to the bookshelf, the spines of fantasy novels staring back at me—a reminder that sometimes escape only lasted as long as a story's pages.

Turning to the window, the sky outside was glaringly bright, a beautiful, defiant blue that mocked my stormy mind. I took a steadying breath and turned back to my bed, tossing clothes haphazardly into a worn duffel bag. Running away might not be a solution, but staying felt impossible.

My phone buzzed on the bed, its vibrations rippling through the comforter. Probably Dean again. Or maybe Regi or someone from work—each a link in the chain tethering me to a life that felt like it was strangling me.

"Not now," I muttered, tossing the phone aside. I zipped the bag shut with a finality that felt decisive. Slinging it over my shoulder, I closed my eyes, hearing only the faint hum of my laptop, the muffled city sounds beyond the window, and the quiet echo of Dean's voice. I had taken a step, however small, and it was enough.

Downstairs, the roar of my car's engine filled the air, the faint smell of gasoline mixing with the delicate perfume of blooming flowers from the nearby park. I watched an old woman pass by, pushing a stroller, laughter and soft conversations drifting toward me—sounds from a world I was no longer part of.

I slipped into the passenger seat, the weight of my solitude suddenly overwhelming. Who would listen to me, really listen? My chest tightened, but I shook it off, climbed back into the driver's seat, and set the GPS for Santa Cruz. Mickey. We hadn't spoken in years, but maybe some bonds were resilient enough to survive the passage of time.

The road blurred as I drove, the hum of the engine and the miles stretching out like lifelines in the night. Six hours later, I arrived in front of Mickey's house. I rang the bell, and when he opened the door, his expression shifted from shock to warmth.

"You drove here from Vegas?" he asked, his eyebrows raised.

"Would you believe me if I said I hitchhiked?" I joked, a half-smile tugging at my lips.

He chuckled, pulling me into a hug. "It's good to see you, man. Come on in."

Inside, the scent of coffee and old books filled the air. We talked late into the night, reminiscing and catching up, the familiar comfort of friendship filling the empty spaces.

The next day, Mickey suggested I take a temporary job at his friend Carlos's restaurant. The pay was minimal, but it was enough for now. The restaurant smelled of sizzling meat and lime, warm tortillas, and something like home.

But a week later, my phone rang again, and the fragile threads of my new life began to unravel. My mother's voice came through, raw with worry.

"Where are you? We've been worried sick."

"I needed space, Mom. Just some time to think," I said, feeling the old guilt resurface.

"Running away isn't the answer," she said. The truth in her words stung, though I'd known it all along.

Another call came in, this time from my boss. "Can you be back by Monday?" His voice was soft, almost pleading, and the guilt tightened its grip.

I looked at Mickey, who'd overheard the conversation. He gave me a small nod of understanding. "I think it's time to go back," I murmured.

He patted my shoulder. "Yeah. Life waits for no one."

AS HERMES TURNED TO leave, his final words lingered in the air, soft yet potent.

"Family is your anchor. Don't trade it for a ship that promises distant treasures—some ships are destined to be lost at sea." He looked at me, his eyes bright with divine wisdom. "Enjoy this evening, but don't let regret cast a shadow over your choices."

With a final flourish of his winged staff, Hermes vanished, leaving only the faintest ripple of air. I glanced down at the gold coin in my hand, feeling its warmth pulsing in time with my heartbeat. The five-pointed star glowed faintly, a reminder of the balance between the material and the spiritual, a symbol of choices that couldn't be undone.

At that moment, I understood. Family, wealth, identity—all these things were connected, each influencing the other. And it was up to me to decide what held the most value, even if that meant standing at the edge of uncertainty.

The Tarot

The Tarot

Junior held his post by the door, standing with a formal yet inviting air. As each guest arrived, an energetic blend of scents—perfume, cologne, the gentle rustle of fine silks, and soft brocades—floated into the hall. Beside Count Corvin, I greeted each guest, savoring the grace of old-world charm in our gestures.

The servants soon emerged through a discrete door near the kitchen, bearing trays filled with aromatic dishes. A mix of savory scents filled the air as they arranged each course with precision.

Junior cleared his throat. "Ladies and gentlemen, the dining hall is now ready to receive you."

Following him, we made our way down the short corridor connecting the rooms. Even this passageway felt grand, with its frescoed ceilings and ancestral portraits lining the walls, their eyes following us as we moved. As we entered the dining hall, I was struck by the grandeur of the multiple tables laid out with opulent dinnerware and crystal, the chandeliers above casting shimmering patterns across the room. Count Corvin had truly orchestrated an evening of splendor.

I took my seat at the head table beside Count Corvin, with the Gypsy Queen on his other side, her presence radiant in jewel-toned fabrics. Around us sat members of the Major Arcana, each exuding a unique mystique.

Junior reappeared, holding a slender staff with a silver bell, which he rang softly as the first course was presented. "Dinner is served."

JUNIOR LED MAJOR ARCANA toward a second table, his lantern casting flickering shadows along the cobblestone floor. This table was an artful fusion of craftsmanship and mysticism, draped in a tablecloth woven from threads that appeared to be made of moonlight and sunlight. Each chair bore an embroidered cushion adorned with ancient symbols, seemingly chosen to resonate with each Arcana member.

The Hierophant nodded approvingly. "Our seats are spellbound. Thoughtful indeed, young man."

Junior stammered. "Only the best for such esteemed guests."

The Empress gestured toward the centerpiece—a cornucopia spilling with pomegranates, figs, and plums, each fruit a vibrant testament to nature's bounty. "These fruits seem enchanted," she noted.

Junior smiled. "Harvested under the full moon from orchards guarded by ancient sentinels, each piece is imbued with the elements. They nourish both body and spirit."

The Devil chuckled. "So, they enhance our powers?"

"Precisely," Junior replied, relieved by the positive reception.

The Fool winked at Junior. "You've done well. Sometimes, the setting is as essential as the players themselves."

Flushed with pride, Junior left the room as the Arcana delved into discussions on the magic of creation and destruction.

IN ANOTHER PART OF the hall, I watched Junior as he seated the House of Wands. Prometheus, a tall figure with a piercing gaze, looked at Junior with a hint of amusement. "Your orchestration is almost as refined as the harpist's touch," he remarked.

Junior offered a modest smile. "Thank you, Lord Prometheus. I aimed to ensure everything was to your liking."

"Did you choreograph the candlelight to flicker with your own nerves?" Prometheus teased, and a ripple of laughter spread.

Junior's face reddened, but Queen Seraphina leaned over to offer reassurance. "You've done beautifully, Junior. We're all grateful."

He straightened his shoulders, a spark of confidence igniting within him. "Thank you, Your Grace. It's an honor to serve."

The Knight, Sir Cedric, raised his goblet. "To Junior, the evening's quiet hero."

"Hear, hear!" echoed the Page, Elara, a fiery young woman with a quick wit.

Junior beamed, feeling both humbled and proud as he retreated to his duties.

MARY MAGDALEN AND HER entourage, the House of Cups, arrived with an air of grace. Junior guided them to their table, where a delicate fountain served as the centerpiece, its gentle waters casting a serene ambiance. The chalice next to the fountain drew Mary Magdalen's attention.

"An evocative piece," Junior said softly. "Its blend of gold and wine speaks of history and reverence."

Mary Magdalen nodded. "Indeed, the weight of history lives within that chalice. It calls us to reflect."

Lady Elspeth murmured, "It reminds us of life's duality—the joy and sorrow interwoven within."

Lord Edmund agreed. "A gathering's essence lies in its capacity to both celebrate and remember."

As the house members took their seats, each seemed to partake in a silent ritual, their gestures echoing generations of shared emotion and reflection.

JUNIOR LED THE HOUSE of Swords, guided by the formidable Takauji, toward their table. Takauji, with his samurai entourage, carried an aura of quiet strength. Their table was adorned with inked scrolls of samurai lore and a mesmerizing centerpiece: a magnetic base that held spinning swords in mid-air, embodying the calm and fury of their craft.

Junior's question hung in the air like the swords themselves: "Master Takauji, how does a blade's craftsmanship reflect its spirit?"

Takauji's eyes narrowed, then softened. "A blade's soul lies in its forging. Every fold and strike is a prayer, a communion with the heavens."

Another samurai added, "Blessed waters quench the metal, imparting a spirit into the sword."

Takauji nodded. "Each blade is a testament to its creator's art and devotion. You honor us by asking, Junior."

IN YET ANOTHER WING, Junior welcomed the House of Pentacles, their table adorned with a living tree, its branches dripping with shimmering coins. Hermes, the trickster god, was among them, casting a smirk at Junior, whose wrists bore small springs—a prank from Hermes himself.

"Remind me to have a word with Hermes later," Junior muttered as he plucked the springs off his cuffs.

The air around the Pentacles table held a distinct energy, almost cooler, denser as if weighted by the ancient knowledge of those gathered. Hermes caught my eye and grinned, lifting his glass.

"Prince Aaron, do you like our Tree of Prosperity? A limited edition," he quipped, clearly delighted by the display.

Junior leaned in. "Be wary of Hermes, Your Highness. Appearances can be deceiving."

Nodding, I marveled at the intricate design before us—a blend of roots and branches symbolizing wealth's complexities and the grounding of ambition.

THE HALL HUMMED WITH layered conversations and laughter, a meeting of kingdoms and realms that felt like the merging of worlds. Each table represented an entire philosophy, an ethos woven into the rich tapestry of this gathering.

Above us, an ethereal chandelier of bioluminescent spores floated, casting a dreamlike glow across the room. Aromas mingled in the air—the herbal freshness of the Druids, the ozone from the Stormbringers, and faint citrus from spells conjured by Alchemists.

As I felt the weight of the night press upon me, Junior appeared by my side with a drink of swirling aquamarine and gold. "Thought you might need this, Your Highness."

I took a grateful sip, feeling calm wash over me. "Thank you, Junior. I don't know how you do it."

He winked. "We all have our roles, Your Highness. Yours is to lead. Mine is to know when you need support."

This wasn't merely a grand event; it was a confluence of lives, a web of alliances, ambitions, and memories. Inhaling deeply, I realized this was my place—to navigate this realm and its connections.

⁂

AS THE FINAL COURSE was cleared, Count Corvin rose, signaling us toward the ballroom. He led the way, his steps echoing in the silence that fell as the doors swung open to reveal a new world beyond.

Inside the ballroom, enchantment took flight. Guests showcased extraordinary feats, blending acrobatics with magic. A woman in Victorian attire transformed into many butterflies before reassembling into her human form. A samurai defied gravity, leaping in breathtaking maneuvers. Hermes himself took to the air on ethereal wings while Prometheus spun spheres of fire in dazzling arcs.

This wasn't merely a celebration. It was a convergence of possibility and imagination—a testament to the art of wonder itself.

As I stood amidst this kaleidoscope of marvels, I realized that tonight was a threshold. It was a rite of passage, a stepping stone toward my own fate.

Taking a steadying breath, I knew I was ready. I had found my place among the stars in this extraordinary cosmos, and tonight, I was not just a participant but a part of the very magic that bound us all.

The Reading

The hardwood floor groaned beneath my boots as I walked alongside Count Corvin, Günter, and Matt. Each step echoed through the cavernous ballroom, where the amber glow of chandeliers lit up walls adorned with velvet tapestries depicting tales of old. The mingled scents of incense and spiced wine added a heady mystique, charging the air with an almost sacred anticipation.

As we reached the center of the room, a gathering of the Tarot awaited us. The Gypsy Queen's sapphire eyes glimmered beneath her veils, Prometheus stood tall and powerful with the weight of ages etched on his face, and Mary Magdalen was a vision of poise and grace. Ashikaga Takauji wore the traditional garb of a samurai, and Hermes the trickster was present as well, his quicksilver gaze taking in every detail.

The Gypsy Queen spoke first. "My Lord, how would you like this reading to proceed?"

Count Corvin inclined his head. "I ask each of you to draw from your knowledge of the cards to guide him through memories obscured. Only by understanding his past can he face his future."

Prometheus stepped forward, his expression solemn. "Such a reading will take time, and it may overwhelm him. The truths uncovered are rarely gentle."

"I need him to face his past without fear," the Count replied. "He's been with me for a year, and in that time, he has found happiness. Haven't you, Aaron?"

"I have," I replied. "Though happiness is an elusive creature, isn't it?"

Mary Magdalen shuffled her cards with a steady hand, saying, "True happiness endures even the scars it carries." Her words lingered, deepening the room's stillness.

Count Corvin's gaze softened as it rested on me. "That's why we're here. My Prince must understand his journey so he can make a choice—for his future and ours."

Suddenly, a young woman stepped forward, fierce and unflinching. "This is not the path you should walk!" she declared. "I have brought Elder Anastasia here to ensure this reading remains just. Fate twists when bent to human will."

The Count's eyes narrowed. "You challenge this rite, Justice? I don't have another year to wait. We are on the brink."

Justice's voice was steady. "Fate is not bound to urgency, Count. For this to be true and just, it must be impartial." Tall and formidable, her armor gleamed with a brilliance that seemed almost otherworldly. Her breastplate bore the insignia of balanced scales, and she held a sword pointed skyward, a symbol of truth and unwavering judgment.

The young woman met my eyes, and there was a flash of something achingly familiar. "My name is Ximena. This man is Aaron, my brother. He disappeared into shadows a year ago, and I want him back—whole, not as some relic of your desires, but as he was: flawed, human, mine."

Count Corvin turned to her with a penetrating look. "You're not here alone, are you?"

Ximena's gaze didn't waver. "No. Günter captured our brother Manuel as he searched for me. I demand his release."

The Count's mask of control slipped. "If what you say is true, then this changes matters greatly." He gestured toward Günter, whose eyes held a flicker of disdain.

"Günter, release Manuel and see he is taken to the guest quarters," the Count ordered.

Ximena's eyes turned to Matt. "I would prefer Matt attend to him," she insisted. "Günter has earned no trust from us."

I stepped forward. "Matt will see to Manuel."

Count Corvin glanced at me, and the weight of his gaze softened as he pulled me close. "For a year, you've been my beloved Prince. Today, you are also Aaron." His words lingered between us, both an acknowledgment and an invitation.

Ximena added, "For this reading to be true, I request the guidance of a Seer, one versed in the Major Arcana and the four suits."

At that, a new figure entered the room, an elderly woman with silver hair like spun frost and eyes bright with wisdom. "I am Elder Anastasia, the Seer," she said. "I've walked these paths many times, through shadow and light. Shall we proceed?"

In that moment, the ballroom felt like a vast theater of fate, where each of us became symbols and stories, entangled in something far greater than ourselves.

"Ximena," the Count began, "You've breached a sacred space. Your brother's captivity is a consequence of your own choices, yet here you seek to rewrite his destiny with magic."

Ximena's gaze didn't falter. "My brother and I seek answers, as you have. We've used every resource to uncover what happened. Can you truly blame us for that?"

The Count was silent for a moment. "Very well, we proceed as planned. The reading will begin with the suits—the Cups, Swords, Wands, and Pentacles. We will then move to the Major Arcana. Let it be known," he said, turning to the Seer, "only the Seer may object to any part of this reading."

The Seer nodded solemnly. "The cards will speak their truth. It shall not be warped by desire or fear."

Count Corvin looked at me, his gaze intense yet tender. "A year together, but you've been a mystery—a mystery we'll unravel tonight."

All eyes turned to the Seer as she prepared the deck, each card a doorway into the soul's hidden realms.

MANUEL'S EYES HELD a fire tempered by pain as he looked at me. "The Günters shouldn't walk this earth, Aaron. They deserve justice." His voice was rough and raw with emotion.

Ximena put a gentle hand on his shoulder. "He doesn't remember, Manuel. Trauma has erased parts of his memory."

I turned to Manuel, studying his face, his familiar yet distant presence. "We used to fight, didn't we? Stupid arguments—our own little game." Then, turning to Ximena, I said, "And Santino...he always found his way into my bed, no matter where he was supposed to sleep."

Ximena's voice softened. "Yes. You're thirty, Manuel is twenty-seven, I'm nineteen, and Santino is seventeen. You raised us, Aaron. Now it's our turn to bring you home."

Matt's face was grim. "Escape won't be easy. Günter's guards have orders to kill anyone matching your description."

Matt's words were interrupted by the toll of a bell. "The Eleventh Hour," he said. "My Lord, it's time for your reading. Ximena, stay with Manuel. I'll escort Aaron."

Manuel gave a weak but defiant grin. "Just don't make this any more dramatic than it has to be," he muttered, and Ximena smiled.

As she embraced me, her touch was grounding. A piece of home in a world turned strange.

COUNT CORVIN'S GRIP on Ximena's neck was vicious, his fingers pressing into her skin as his fangs emerged. "You and your brothers are meddling with forces beyond your understanding," he hissed, his voice like ice.

"My Lord," I said, gripping his wrist, meeting his dark gaze without flinching. "This is not the time for threats."

After a tense pause, he released her, and I pulled Ximena back. Matt guided us down a dark corridor leading to the dungeon—a place of agony and fear, reeking of decay.

We found Manuel chained to a grim device, his body contorted and bleeding. His eyes met mine, a fleeting recognition before pain overtook him.

Ximena gasped. "What have they done to him?"

Matt had been tending to him. "I've done what I can here, but he needs proper care."

I nodded. "Take him to my chambers, Matt. Do whatever it takes to keep him alive."

Manuel's gaze hardened. "The Günters will pay for this, Aaron. But for now, it's enough to see you're alive."

Overwhelmed, I searched his face for memories that were just out of reach. "Someone is missing, isn't there? Another sibling?"

Ximena's voice cracked. "Yes, but that's a story for another time. Right now, we need to get Manuel to safety."

In that dark, foul place, I felt the weight of family, of loyalties tangled and painfully real. This was my life—a life I couldn't fully remember, yet one that pulled at me with the force of forgotten love and shared blood.

A CRY IN THE NIGHT woke me. I walked down the dimly lit hallway, the scent of my mother's cinnamon incense still lingering in the air. When I reached Ximena's door, I found her tiny form huddled in her crib, milk dripping from an overturned bottle.

"What's wrong, sweetie?" I whispered, lifting her gently. Her little hands gripped mine as her cries softened. I felt her warmth and weight in my arms, a reminder of the quiet acts of care that hold families together.

I cleaned the crib, wiped down the mattress, and changed her clothes, soothing her as she whimpered. Her tiny face gradually relaxed, her breathing slowing to gentle little sighs. I laid her back down in the fresh sheets, tucking her in. She gazed at me with drowsy eyes before closing them, finally at peace. I watched her fall into a deep, contented sleep, feeling a profound sense of home wrap itself around me—a home built from small, tender moments, each one binding us closer, one thread at a time.

MATT INTERRUPTED MY reverie. "Prince Aaron, it's time."

I turned to Ximena. "Will you come with us?"

She hesitated, glancing around the opulent yet dark halls. "Yes. I want to remember this place as it is now before it changes forever."

As we moved down the corridor, I felt the weight of my lost memories and the promise of answers. Whatever awaited me in the reading, I knew that this time, I wouldn't be facing it alone. And that knowledge, however fragile, was enough.

The Horoscope Reading

Stepping into the grand hall, a sense of charged anticipation enveloped me. The air was thick with the fragrance of freshly cut flowers intermingled with the warm, spicy aroma of incense. Conversations hummed softly, an undercurrent to the room's grandeur. The hall itself was a marvel, with seats arranged in a semicircular formation that focused all eyes on Count Corvin's throne, perched atop Grecian pillars. The throne was a masterpiece of crimson velvet embroidered in gold thread, catching the flickering candlelight in a mesmerizing dance.

Count Corvin met me with a graceful flourish, taking my hand to lead me to the throne. A slight smile touched his lips as I settled onto the ornate seat. Elder Anastasia, the Seer, appeared beside me, her presence lending a palpable mystique to the ceremony.

The horoscope reading began. Each station brought a revelation, peeling back layers of my past, present, and future. Elder Anastasia's voice was both firm and gentle as she guided me through questions and insights.

"Let us begin with the core of your essence," she said, her tone reflective yet unyielding. "Who are you, Prince Aaron? What drives you? What secrets lie in the depths of your soul?"

I took a breath. "I am a Prince, yes, but I'm also a seeker—of truth, of purpose. My soul craves adventure, knowledge, and a deeper understanding of the world."

Elder Anastasia nodded. We moved through each zodiac station, uncovering facets of my personality and destiny, from adaptability to thought processes, exploring how these qualities intertwined with my relationships. Each card was an unmasking, offering reflections I'd scarcely considered.

Finally, Elder Anastasia turned to me, her gaze as sharp as it was ancient. "Prince Aaron, the Significator shall guide you through the veils of time and destiny."

My heart beat faster as her words settled on me. "But what is this Significator?" I asked.

The Gypsy Queen, who had been watching, smiled enigmatically. "The Significator is more than a guide. It will channel your thoughts, access your memories, and help reveal the tapestry of your past, present, and future."

As she spoke, the four Knights gathered around her. Each Knight bore the symbols of the elements that held sway over our kingdom: fire, water, earth, and air.

THE KNIGHT OF PENTACLES, a young man with golden hair, stepped forward, holding a large coin engraved with an intricate pentacle. His steady voice matched his composed demeanor. "I am the Knight of Pentacles."

He embodied the essence of time's steady flow, a figure of discipline and quiet strength. "Time is like a river, Prince Aaron," he said, his words measured. "I am grounded, constant, and patient."

I inclined my head, absorbing his presence. "Even the strongest river can be swayed by external forces. What might threaten to throw us off course?"

The Knight's expression softened. "Life is full of distractions, desires, and unforeseen challenges. These forces can distort our perception of time, leading us astray."

His words resonated with me, bringing to mind times I'd been pulled from my path. "My role as your Significator is to remind you of your core values, grounding you in the present, even as you face echoes of the past and glimpses of the future."

The Knight of Cups then stepped forward, his vibrant red hair flowing like a river of flame, clothed in a flowing white tunic beneath a rich red robe. He held a cup decorated with intertwined serpents, his expression both intense and serene.

"I am the Knight of Cups," he declared, his voice lyrical. "I embody the spirit of adventure and the longing for recognition, yet I also seek harmony and peace."

"How do you balance ambition with peace?" I asked, intrigued.

He smiled gently. "Balance is the ultimate pursuit. Ambition and tranquility are not opposites but partners. Together, they create harmony."

I knew his words would linger with me, a reminder to find peace even in pursuit. "As your Significator, I will guide you through ambition and longing, helping you find that delicate balance."

THE THIRD KNIGHT APPROACHED, a centaur with the torso of a man and the powerful lower body of a horse, his chestnut beard and mane flowing like embers in the air. He carried a wand that seemed to spark with energy, and his shield bore symbols of justice and valor.

"I am the Knight of Wands," he announced, his voice like rolling thunder. "I am a force of action and swift decision."

His intense presence made me pause. "Tell me, how do you keep your zeal for justice in check?"

The Knight's laughter was hearty, like a roaring fire. "Justice without restraint is as destructive as unchecked fire. Passion must be tempered with wisdom. I've seen what unbridled action can destroy."

He paced hooves echoing through the hall. "I am here to remind you of the need for balance. Your passion for justice must be balanced by compassion."

His words struck a deep chord within me. I understood that his presence would guide me, showing that justice demanded not just action but compassion.

FINALLY, THE KNIGHT of Swords approached, dressed in regal Asian robes adorned with intricate patterns. His sword, a long katana, was sheathed at his side, and a half-moon symbol graced his headgear. His presence commanded respect.

"I am the Knight of Swords," he said, his voice sharp and authoritative. "The sword is my truth, but even truth must be wielded with care."

"Knight of Swords," I said, "how do you balance the pursuit of justice with restraint?"

He unsheathed his sword slightly, the torchlight glinting off the steel. "Justice is sacred, but excessive force can tarnish its purity. I have learned to weigh each action carefully, measuring aggression against necessity."

He returned his sword to its sheath. "I will be your guide, showing you the strength of restraint and the wisdom of discernment."

Together, the four Knights represented the forces that shaped me, a quartet of values that encapsulated my character and aspirations.

THE KNIGHTS STOOD AS one, their voices blending in solemn unity. "We, the Knights of Pentacles, Cups, Wands, and Swords, commit to guiding you through this reading with fairness and justice."

The Gypsy Queen's eyes met mine. "Prince Aaron, this reading will unfold in three spreads. We shall begin with the Horoscope, a layout of twelve cards, to explore the celestial influences shaping you now."

Each card, she explained, would reveal a layer of my existence, shedding light on influences both hidden and apparent. I felt a thrill of curiosity mixed with caution as I reached for the first card.

But before I could draw, Elder Anastasia intervened. "Gypsy Queen, I advise restraint tonight. A single spread of the Horoscope will suffice."

The Gypsy Queen's gaze turned icy, though her tone remained calm. I sensed the tension between these two mystics, each bearing a different philosophy of the mystical world.

The Gypsy Queen turned back to me, her expression softening. "Prince Aaron, the Horoscope shall serve as our map. Let us draw the first card and begin."

AS I PREPARED TO DRAW, I felt the weight of their collective intent. I reached for the card, and with the flickering torchlight casting shifting shadows across the intricate artwork, I began my journey into the depths of fate.

With the Knights and the Seer beside me, each card I drew would reveal another layer of my destiny, illuminated by the ancient wisdom of the stars. The journey had only begun, but I was ready, bolstered by the Knights' strength and the Seer's guidance, to navigate the unfolding mysteries of the cosmos.

Position 1 House of Identity

The grand hall felt charged, like a cauldron simmering with untapped power. Each tapestry was a spell, each scent a potion, each chant an echo of ancient summoning. Elder Anastasia's voice rose with the resonance of incense smoke, grounding her question with unmistakable gravity.

"Who will take the position of the House of Identity, the First House?"

Her words stretched across the silence, weighted with expectation. For a moment, time itself seemed to hold its breath. No one stepped forward, and the chanting morphed into an eerie, rhythmic drone that heightened the suspense.

A faint rustling broke through the quiet—a whisper of ancient parchment piercing the thick atmosphere.

"I, the Hanged Man, shall assume this role," a voice declared.

A figure materialized, emerging from the shadows and walking forward with deliberate, weighty steps. The noose around his neck swayed, moving with the cadence of his stride. His gaze, bloodshot and piercing, locked onto mine as he reached the center of the room. Without ceremony, he lifted the noose from his neck and let it fall to the floor, revealing marks around his throat. His attire was simple yet dignified: tan slacks and a plain black shirt.

"Prince Aaron," he intoned, kneeling before me with an intensity that felt almost tangible.

"I embody your paradoxes and the hidden facets of your soul. I wear the noose as you wear your many masks—not as a symbol of restraint but as a reminder of the delicate balance between struggle and liberation."

His words struck me deeply. Here, he was saying that even the masks I wore—the ones I used to hide or protect myself—were part of my truth. They weren't lies but facets of my identity.

"So, you're saying that my masks aren't deception but rather parts of who I am?"

"Precisely, My Prince," the Hanged Man affirmed, rising to his feet. "These masks are layers of you. Each serves a purpose, whether to guard, reveal, or obscure. The key is to wear them with intention rather than letting them define you."

Elder Anastasia nodded in approval. "The House of Identity has found its first guardian. Let us continue." She gestured to the remaining Tarot cards, still turned face down.

The Hanged Man's gaze remained on me, his presence unwavering. "I represent the fragments of your identity you've lost or hidden, pieces of yourself scattered across the landscapes of your past."

As he spoke, a subtle light seemed to focus on him, illuminating his words with a quiet reverence. My pulse quickened as I listened, each phrase resonating within me.

"You often play the role of the sacrificial lamb, craving acceptance yet fearing rejection. When others turn away, the hollowness within echoes, amplifying the emptiness."

His words were like a mirror, reflecting not just my outer self but the intricacies of my inner landscape—sharp peaks and dark valleys shaped by the erosion of time and experience.

"You are the mirror that reflects my own soul's complexities," I murmured, struck by his truth. "You remind me that even in struggle and sacrifice, there is the potential for self-discovery."

The Hanged Man nodded. As he stepped back, I glanced down and saw that the noose at his feet had dissolved into the floor, leaving no trace.

Elder Anastasia broke the silence. "The House of Identity has its first guardian, Prince Aaron. Are you ready to confront what awaits in the next house?"

I took a steadying breath. "Yes, I'm ready."

STEPPING OUT OF THE office building into the brisk evening air, I felt the weight of the day lift from my shoulders. Fatigue clung to me, but it was overpowered by an undercurrent of excitement—I'd just been promoted to management, complete with a four percent raise.

I slid into my car, the leather seats cool beneath me, and my mind jumped ahead to the new possibilities. With this raise, I could finally afford that sleek charcoal-gray sedan I'd been eyeing at the dealership. I could already imagine myself behind its wheel.

First, though, I made a quick stop at Hassim's Convenience Store. The air inside was warm, tinged with the scent of fresh coffee and pre-packaged sandwiches.

"Hey, Aaron! How's it going?" Hassim called from behind the counter, a welcoming smile on his face.

"Great, Hassim—really great!" I replied, unable to keep the grin from my face. "Pack of Marlboros, please."

"Special occasion?" he asked, sliding the cigarettes toward me.

"Yeah, I just got promoted!"

"Congratulations!" he beamed. "This one's on the house."

I laughed, tucking the cigarettes into my pocket. "I'll remember this when I'm CEO!"

Back in my car, I allowed myself a quiet moment of triumph before heading home. When I finally pulled into our driveway, I took a moment to savor the sight of our modest family home, glowing warmly in the twilight.

Inside, I was greeted by the comforting aroma of my mom's famous pot roast. The murmur of the TV drifted in from the living room, where Dad was probably watching the evening news. But I wanted a moment of solitude before sharing my news, so I slipped out to the backyard.

Lighting a cigarette, I took a long drag, watching the smoke rise into the darkening sky. The cool air was grounding, enhancing my sense of gratitude. Tomorrow, I will enter the office with a new title and new responsibilities. Still, for now, it was just me, the sky, and a feeling of quiet fulfillment.

AS THE SETTING SUN bathed the backyard in a warm, amber glow, my father's rabbits darted around, hopping with the unbridled joy of tiny Olympians. I watched them from our worn wooden picnic table, savoring the moment. Twenty-two rabbits, each with its own quirks and energy.

Lighting a cigarette, I let the taste of tobacco mix with the musky smell of the rabbits and the lingering warmth of the afternoon. My reverie was interrupted by my brother Manuel's voice.

"Aaron," he said, his tone measured.

"Yeah?" I answered, eyes still on the rabbits.

"Our father's sister and her family are on their way."

"Oh, nice. It's been a while since I last saw them."

Manuel hesitated, his voice edged with tension. "Before they arrive, I need you gone. We don't need the embarrassment."

The words hit like a slap, familiar yet freshly wounding. This wasn't the first time Manuel wanted me out of sight when family visited, as if my presence—my very identity—could somehow tarnish him.

Clenching my cigarette tighter, I managed a nod. "I'll let Mom know I'm heading out."

I stubbed out my cigarette and walked into the house, feeling the warmth turn stifling. In the kitchen, Mom's hands were busy with a mixing bowl.

"I'm heading out," I said, keeping my tone light.

She looked up, concern flickering in her eyes. "Everything okay?"

"Yeah, I just need some air."

Back in my car, I sat gripping the steering wheel, my mind a storm of frustration and hurt. Without thinking, I pressed my foot harder on the gas, hurtling down the winding roads, feeling a desperate, reckless pull toward oblivion.

But then, faces flashed through my mind—friends who had become my chosen family, people at work who respected me for who I was. They reminded me I wasn't alone, even if my own blood struggled to accept me. Gradually, I eased my foot off the gas, reclaiming control over the car and my emotions. I couldn't change my family's expectations, but I could choose to live beyond their limits.

LATER THAT NIGHT, I found myself parked in Regi's driveway, the air cold as I lit another cigarette. The smoke curled upward, a pale ribbon against the night sky. Just then, headlights swept across the driveway. Regi stepped out of her car, her piercing blue eyes immediately finding mine, concern etched on her face.

"Aaron, what's going on? Why are you here?" she asked, pulling me into a warm embrace. My walls crumbled, and I felt tears spill over.

"Come inside," she said softly. "I'll make us some tea."

In her cozy, slightly cluttered kitchen, the scent of jasmine floated through the air. Regi's calm presence filled the room as she set about making tea, moving with the easy grace of someone who understood.

As she poured the tea, she finally spoke. "Did you quit your job?"

I shook my head. "No... it's just my family. Manuel made it clear he didn't want me around while the relatives visited."

She set down her teacup with a soft thud. "That's awful, Aaron. But remember, that doesn't define you."

"It's just... sometimes it feels like it does."

Regi leaned forward, her gaze steady. "Then rise above it. Don't let their narrow view cage you. You have people who love and value you."

The warmth of her words and her belief in me softened the ache. I took a deep breath, feeling a small but steady strength return.

<hr>

BACK IN THE GRAND HALL, The Hanged Man's figure loomed large, his presence inescapable. His noose had dissolved, but his message lingered.

"The masks you wear, Prince Aaron—they guard you, but they also separate you." His voice was calm yet penetrating.

Elder Anastasia's gaze was firm. "The Hanged Man speaks of sacrifice, yes, but also of perspective. To see the world from a new angle, you must let go of pretense."

I felt the weight of their words settles on my shoulders. My masks were shields, but they were also prisons, keeping me from my truest self.

"Am I protecting myself with these masks, or just running from who I really am?" I asked, more to myself than anyone else.

"Only you can answer that," Elder Anastasia replied. "But know this—sometimes, to truly see, we must allow ourselves to hang in the uncertainty."

In that room, surrounded by the wisdom of The Hanged Man and the silent strength of Elder Anastasia, I felt something shift. Perhaps it was time to see myself not just through others' eyes but through my own, stripped of the masks and layers I'd hidden behind.

Position 2 House of Change

The room was a silent amphitheater, and each figure around me was a rapt witness as Elder Anastasia took her place on the raised dais at the center. Her gaze swept over us, settling momentarily on me before moving to the others.

"It is time for the second representative to assume their place in the House of Change," her voice reverberated through the grand hall. "The House of Change is not just about how the world acts upon us, but how we choose to act in return. The representative must embody survival, resilience, and transformation—strength in both mind and body."

All eyes fixed on a shadowy figure that seemed to materialize out of thin air, cloaked in a dark, flowing tunic that seemed to absorb the surrounding light.

"I shall take this role," the figure declared. Its voice was layered, both male and female, ethereal yet unmistakably clear. A skeletal hand, its bones faintly glowing against the surrounding darkness, emerged from beneath the robe and gripped a scythe that gleamed ominously in the dim light.

"I am Death, the embodiment of inevitable change," the figure proclaimed, "Adaptation is my power. While you may not control change itself, how you respond is forever within your command."

Elder Anastasia looked between Death and me, her expression intrigued. "Death has never before chosen to assume a role in the House of Change. Your presence here is... unprecedented."

"Unprecedented but essential," Death replied, turning its hooded face toward her. "Strength is not always found in resistance. Sometimes, surrender to the inevitable—facing it with courage—is the truest form of resilience."

As Death advanced, it extended the scythe toward me. "Take this instrument and reflect upon the transformations you have endured. Consider how you've responded to the tides of life."

I reached out, gripping the cold steel and ancient wood of the scythe. The instant I touched it, a flood of sensations washed over me—a paradoxical calm that felt like a pearl of shared wisdom, as though Death itself were revealing the nature of change.

Elder Anastasia's voice broke the silence. "Then it is decided. Death will occupy the role of the House of Change, the second in line."

Death bowed its head, intoning, "And so it is."

RIA HAD BEEN A CONSTANT presence in my life, a resilient young woman whose spirit matched her strength. Through the years we shared in school, she became my confidante, partner-in-crime, and fellow advocate for change. Together, we pushed boundaries in Student Government, rallying for events and policy shifts with a conviction that earned us both admiration and envy.

One privilege from our shared efforts was a trip to Virginia City, a town steeped in history. In the midst of its antique shops and cobblestone streets, Ria and I picked out postcards, laughing as she playfully kissed each one I planned to send to friends, leaving lipstick marks and the words "Wish you were here."

Back at school a few days later, though, the prank didn't land as harmlessly as we'd intended. My roommate Patrick held up his postcard, studying it with mock disapproval as he paced across our dorm's worn carpet.

"I fail to see the humor," he remarked, the heel of his cowboy boots scraping the floor with each step. "Seems like a prank that backfired."

"It was Ria's idea," I insisted, picturing her laughing in the tiny post office as she planted those kisses on each card.

Patrick glanced at me and shrugged, letting it slide, but Doug, another friend, was less forgiving. Tall and lean, his thick glasses magnified his discontent as he brandished his own postcard.

"Frankly, it's offensive," Doug fumed. "Imagine sending a card with me as the Silver Queen! It's unacceptable."

"It was meant to be lighthearted," I replied, hoping to defuse the tension. "We didn't mean to offend anyone."

Doug studied me for a moment, then gave a dismissive wave. "Next time, maybe think twice before being so impulsive."

Patrick rolled his eyes, a faint smile softening his stance. "Sounds like classic Ria. Given that you're holding Death's scythe now, we'll let it pass this time."

※

THE POSTCARD INCIDENT seemed to spiral into something beyond my control. Later that day, I was summoned to the Student Government counselor's office, the long hallway stretching before me like a march toward judgment.

Mr. Thompson, the counselor, sat behind his mahogany desk, stacks of papers surrounding him. The room smelled of stale coffee, and the fluorescent lights buzzed faintly overhead, casting a harsh glow.

"Sit down, Aaron," he said, gesturing to the chair across from him.

The stern look on his face made my heart sink.

"The postcard incident has escalated," he began. "People are calling for action."

"It was just a misunderstanding," I protested.

He sighed. "Perhaps, but the school can't afford a scandal. Effective immediately, you're expelled from Student Government." His words struck like a blow, but he continued, "You're also suspended from the Big Brother, Big Sister program."

The weight of his decision settled over me, stripping me of the roles and privileges I'd worked so hard to earn. I returned to my dorm to find Patrick packing his belongings.

"Looks like we're not roommates anymore," he said, his voice flat.

"Yeah." It was all I could manage in response.

Doug passed by our open door, pausing to observe the scene with barely concealed satisfaction.

"So, the mighty have fallen, have they?" he remarked, adjusting his glasses.

"Yes," I said, looking him in the eye. "It's true."

With a smug smile, he turned and walked away. Patrick zipped his bag, casting me a last, unreadable look.

"Take care, Aaron," he said.

"You too, Patrick." I watched him leave, the emptiness settling in as the door clicked shut behind him.

TWO WEEKS LATER, PATRICK slipped into my room unannounced, like a ghost from a life I was still mourning. His presence stirred something unresolved within me.

"You're not supposed to be here," I reminded him, the words more of a defense than a warning.

He ignored my protest, reclining on his old bed, his eyes locked on mine. "I had to say something."

Before I could respond, a tap at the window drew my attention. I saw John standing outside, waiting for me, his expression curious.

I turned back to Patrick, only to find him seizing my shirt and pulling me close until our faces were inches apart.

"You're mine," he said, his voice low and possessive, sending a chill through me.

The words barely registered before he leaned in, his lips brushing mine in a possessive kiss before he released me and strode out of the room, leaving me stunned.

For a moment, I stood frozen, a torrent of emotions raging within me. Patrick had been a significant part of my life, a force of ruin and yet the focus of unspoken feelings. This turn felt like a secret wish brought to life, yet I couldn't ignore the scars he'd left.

Could love, or even the idea of it, justify the risk?

RIA'S CONCERN WAS LIKE a mirror, reflecting the gravity of my decisions. In the library where we had shared countless hours of study and friendship, her eyes shone with unshed tears.

"Aaron, you can't just leave. You're so close to graduation," she implored.

"I don't have a choice, Ria," I replied. "It's either leave now or face expulsion."

She searched my face, desperate for a solution. "What's your plan?"

"The school found me a job with State Unemployment," I explained. "I'll stay with friends for now."

Her expression shifted, tinged with skepticism. "And Patrick? What happens there?"

"He's staying to finish school. He even proposed," I said, the words tasting bitter on my tongue.

She stared at me in disbelief. "Aaron, this is the same person who's hurt you over and over. If you have to leave, go back to Vegas, not to him. He'll only ruin you."

I felt myself bristle. "Patrick promised me things would be different, Ria. Maybe you're just envious."

Her voice rose, raw and fervent. "Envious? Of a relationship that cost you everything? Aaron, I'm not jealous; I'm terrified. You were one of the few openly gay students who found peace here. Don't sacrifice that for someone who's shown you nothing but pain."

Her words cut through the haze of denial. For the first time, I truly saw the crossroads before me: a path leading to ruin or one back to myself.

ELDER ANASTASIA'S GAZE lingered over the Tarot spread before her, her fingers hovering above the cards as though channeling hidden knowledge from each symbol. The air grew colder as Death emerged from his card, his form coalescing, dark robes billowing with an unnatural grace.

"Change lives within you," Death said, his voice resonant and echoing through the grand hall. "It is not imposed but embraced, and your response defines you."

As he spoke, he reclaimed his scythe, the blade gleaming as though lit from within. His dark eyes, voids with twinkling stars, fixed on me with unexpected warmth.

"See me as an end, if you must," he continued, "but know that I am also a beginning. Your emotions are a compass—fear teaches caution, love inspires courage, and sorrow grants wisdom. Let these guide you, not as burdens but as tools to navigate the sea of change."

Elder Anastasia smiled gently. "The cards do not alter the truth; they merely reveal it. What you choose to do with that revelation is yours alone."

Her words, like Death's, settled over me, a reminder that I had the power to shape my destiny if only I dared to embrace the changes that life brought.

Position 3 House of Ideas

Elder Anastasia rose from her seat with a calm, commanding presence, her robes a deep maroon and gold that shimmered like ancient scrolls unfurling around her. She took her place on the elevated platform, her eyes reflecting the wisdom of countless lifetimes as she surveyed the room.

"Who will assume the position of House of Ideas, third in line?" Her voice echoed through the grand hall, each word carrying the weight of ancient tradition. "This role embodies mental resilience, a wellspring of strength and stamina from within. Whoever takes this role must share their approach to sustaining their mind amid life's relentless challenges."

The room, already buzzing with dialogue, grew more animated. Fragments of conversation floated through the air—the Magician discussing the power of focused intent, the Empress extolling the value of compassion, and the Tower and the Fool locked in a spirited debate over the role of chaos and spontaneity in personal growth. Incense thickened the air, and the flickering orbs suspended above seemed to pulse with a new urgency.

A ripple of movement silenced the room as all eyes shifted toward a woman who seemed to materialize within the ceremonial circle, her red curls blazing like a living flame. She wore a skirt fashioned from interlocking silver chains that glimmered as she moved, a tapestry of light and shadow following her every step.

She held a golden chalice in each hand, one filled with water, the other with wine. With a fluid motion, she poured the water into the wine and then the wine into the water, an effortless dance that defied the natural order.

"I am Temperance," she announced, her voice resonant and layered with wisdom beyond measure. "I stand at the crossroads of thought and action, where dreams coalesce into reality."

She tilted the chalices, pouring the blended liquid into a larger cup that waited before her. The liquid shimmered, catching fragments of light that danced like stars within its depths.

"In the fusion of reality and imagination, of material and ethereal, lies the boundless spectrum of possibility. To limit one is to limit them all." Her gaze met mine as she gestured to the chalice.

"Drink, Prince Aaron, and know the alchemy of thoughts becoming actions, of visions shaping reality."

I stepped forward, my heart pounding as I lifted the chalice to my lips. The liquid was cool as it traveled down my throat, settling in my core. It left behind a warmth, a harmony that pulsed through me, merging conflicting facets of myself. I felt a sudden clarity, a sense of thoughts crystallizing into intention, of intentions leaning toward action, each sustaining the other.

As I lowered the chalice, Temperance's gaze held mine. Her voice softened as she spoke.

"Remember this moment, for the realm of ideas is infinite. Only through the harmonious blending of thought and action can you manifest your potential."

With that, she stepped back, her form dissolving into a cascade of light, leaving behind a stillness that seemed to amplify the significance of her message. I rejoined the circle, feeling as though I carried a renewed sense of purpose, the House of Ideas now a vibrant part of my understanding.

THE ROOM WAS DESIGNED to soothe, with framed diplomas and walls painted in calming hues. Yet today, even the lavender and chamomile aroma mingling with the musk of old books felt misplaced in the shadows of my mind.

Dr. Harris sat across from me, her expression both compassionate and analytical. She watched as I stared out the window, my thoughts drifting like raindrops sliding down the glass.

"How did your relationship with Patrick shape your perception of self-worth and success?" she asked gently.

A sigh escaped me as I looked away. "It's complicated. Patrick accused me of something I didn't do. That accusation cost me my job, my reputation, and a part of who I was. Since then, I've been in a constant state of apprehension. Any success feels like a setup for another fall, another betrayal."

She leaned forward, her eyes softening as she listened. "And this fear of cowboys—how does it tie into these fears?"

My hands tightened, my knuckles pale against the tension. "Patrick was a cowboy in every sense—rough, intense, reckless. That mentality represents a kind of toxic masculinity that I find threatening. It's wrapped up with a fear of physical harm, a reminder of arguments that always seemed on the brink of violence."

Dr. Harris nodded, taking notes before setting her pen aside. "Acknowledging fear is the first step in reclaiming control over it. It may seem irrational at times, but every fear has roots in real experiences, and understanding that connection can give you power over it."

Her words hung in the air, each one loosening a knot I'd tied inside myself. "In our future sessions," she continued, "we'll work through these fears. Together, we'll develop coping strategies, and I'll help you reframe success as something safe and fulfilling."

For the first time in what felt like forever, I felt a flicker of hope—a glimmer that my life could become something greater than these old fears.

THE NEUTRAL TONES OF Dr. Harris's office seemed determined to absorb the intensity of my emotions. The faint scent of chamomile tea lingered between us as I sat across from her, hands clenched.

"You mentioned that Air Supply and Garth Brooks trigger painful memories." Her tone was compassionate. "Music can anchor moments in our lives, for better or worse. Can you tell me about it?"

I looked down, my voice barely a whisper. "Those were our songs. They turned ordinary moments into memories. Now they're just reminders—of pain, of loneliness, of a life I can't let go."

She let the silence fill the room, allowing me to process before she continued. "Do you think your struggle to connect with others stems from these memories?"

I nodded, the weight of it settling around me. "Patrick destroyed my sense of trust. How do I open up to others when I've been betrayed so deeply?"

She leaned forward, her gaze unwavering. "It sounds like Patrick left scars, both physically and emotionally. And you mentioned earlier that his behavior reminded you of your father. Would you like to talk about that?"

"My father was the first to make me feel small, like I was never good enough," I replied, my voice barely audible. "He'd call me a loser, and I guess I internalized it. Patrick's words just echoed those same accusations."

She jotted down a note, then looked back at me, her gaze kind. "Many people unconsciously recreate patterns from childhood in adult relationships, but now that you've identified this, you have the power to break it."

She shifted slightly, her voice softening. "You mentioned that Patrick accused you publicly. Was there a defining moment when you realized the extent of his abuse?"

A painful memory surfaced. "Patrick humiliated me in front of others, accusing me of ruining his life. The way he looked at me as if he enjoyed my humiliation..."

Dr. Harris took a deep breath. "Abuse leaves deep wounds, but recognizing those wounds is a vital part of healing. I've noticed you've built physical defenses like weight gain, as well as emotional defenses. These are coping mechanisms, Aaron, but they're also barriers to your freedom."

Her words struck something within me. For so long, I'd hidden behind layers of defense, both visible and invisible.

"We're out of time for today," Dr. Harris said, glancing at the clock. "But next time, we'll talk about how to disarm these defenses, step by step."

As I left her office, a sense of clarity lingered. The road ahead was daunting, but I finally felt there was a path I could follow—one that didn't lead to a dead end.

THE ROOM GLOWED WITH soft light as Temperance took her place again, her presence commanding as she gazed around the circle.

"Fear," she began, her voice calm yet powerful, "is a crucible in which we forge our true selves. Yet, it is essential to recognize the illusions our minds create—illusions that may imprison us."

Her words resonated, rippling through the air like a stone tossed into still water. "Our fears carve paths in our lives," she continued, lifting a cup filled with water. "Yet some fears are mere shadows, illusions that bind us."

With her other hand, she lifted a cup of wine. "To live fully, we must merge intellect with emotion, wisdom with courage."

She poured the contents of both cups into a third, watching as the two liquids merged into one, shimmering with a strange, beautiful glow.

"Do not simply exist within the boundaries of your fears," she urged. "Instead, navigate them, let them become stepping-stones toward your destiny."

Her words hung in the air as she stepped back, her figure dissolving into the shadows. The room was still, each of us absorbing her wisdom.

In that moment, I understood fear may shape us, but it doesn't define us. Only by merging thought and action, fear and courage, could I truly step forward into the life waiting beyond the shadows.

Position 4 House of Children

Elder Anastasia sat at the far end of a dark oak table etched with esoteric runes. Her veil of silver hair framed wise, discerning eyes that drifted thoughtfully across the spread of tarot cards before her.

"Who will assume the position of the fourth house, the House of Children?" Her voice resonated through the grand hall, a melody laced with age-old wisdom. "The House of Children embodies the balance between the inner child and the adult self. It is the ability to view the world through a child's wonder while responding to it with an adult's insight."

Her words resonated within me, sparking a familiar vulnerability, as though a hidden part of myself was being called forth.

The grand hall was a spectacle of majesty, with gilded chandeliers illuminating velvet draperies embroidered in gold. Beneath my feet stretched a handwoven tapestry depicting the storied lineage of my ancestors. The air seemed to hum with anticipation, and a soft murmur spread through the crowd. All eyes turned toward the entrance.

A young child, appearing both ancient and ageless, approached my throne. His eyes were a striking shade of gold, deep and wise beyond years. He walked unaccompanied, and though advisors whispered urgently and guards reached instinctively for their swords, something held them back. There was a power about him that was beyond their realm.

The child ascended the dais and seated himself beside me. The assembly gasped, and in unison, they murmured, "The Sun."

He turned to me, his voice soft yet commanding. "I represent the 'eyes' through which you view the world, Prince Aaron—past, present, and future. I am the lens through which others see your true self."

"Are you real?" I whispered, caught between disbelief and awe.

The child's golden gaze held mine. "I am both a reminder and a reflection," he said. "The Sun illuminates both your inner child and your adult self. These are not opposites but two parts of a whole. You must learn to trust both—to let the child's curiosity and the adult's wisdom exist in harmony."

His words struck a chord deep within me, as if he had articulated a struggle I hadn't fully acknowledged. "Who are you?" I asked.

He smiled, serene and enigmatic. "I am the Sun, manifest in flesh and spirit, here to remind you of the path to unity. The light you seek lies in your ability to perceive the world with both innocence and discernment."

He stood, descending from the dais with a natural grace. As he walked away, the crowd parted their faces, a mixture of reverence and astonishment. Watching him go, I felt a profound clarity settle over me. Could the simplicity and curiosity of childhood coexist with the demands of adulthood?

"Trust both sides of yourself," he had said. At that moment, I understood that my journey wasn't about choosing between these aspects but embracing them both. In the midst of the assembly's buzzing whispers, I felt an inner transformation. It wasn't a solution to life's complexities but a shift in perspective—a realization that I didn't have to choose between innocence and experience. I could be both.

ANA AND I SAT TOGETHER on a worn, well-loved couch in my modest apartment, the scent of freshly brewed coffee mingling with the sweet, tangy aroma of an apple pie cooling on the windowsill. Afternoon sunlight cast a warm, golden glow through the gauzy curtains, painting intricate patterns on the wooden floor.

Ana eyed me, her gaze sharp yet gentle. "Aaron, something's bothering you, isn't it?"

I hesitated, then sighed, running a hand through my hair. "My thirtieth birthday is coming up, and I've been... well, contemplating."

"Contemplating what?" she pressed, her tone both curious and concerned.

With a small grin, I said, "If you could help me get a fake ID, I could pass as twenty-one again. Think anyone would notice?"

Ana laughed, her eyes widening in mock horror. "Aaron, you're about to turn thirty, not eighteen!"

"Well," I joked, "maybe twenty-one would be more believable."

She shook her head, chuckling. "Why this sudden urge to be twenty-one again?"

I looked down. "Because... because I feel like I've achieved nothing. No real career, just a string of random jobs, no long-term partner. I'm still living at home. This isn't where I thought I'd be by thirty."

Ana's expression softened. "I'm nearly thirty myself, and you don't see me panicking."

"But you're content," I replied. "You've never had these... expectations weighing on you."

Ana shrugged, her gaze steady. "Maybe because I'm learning that life doesn't come with a checklist. It comes with experiences."

WHEN MY BIRTHDAY FINALLY arrived, I chose to focus on celebrating my younger brother's sixteenth birthday instead. We transformed my apartment into a haven of laughter, filling it with pizza, an assortment of movies, and the warmth of youth. As his friends gathered and laughter filled the air, I found myself celebrating a simpler time.

Toward the end of the night, I felt a familiar presence at my side. The ageless child—the Sun—had returned, his golden eyes gleaming with understanding.

"Celebrating someone else's youth doesn't erase your own," he whispered. "To merge your child self and adult self is to free yourself from both."

As he disappeared into the shadows, his words lingered. Could I reconcile the dreams of my younger self with the realities of adulthood? Could I accept that my life, though imperfect, was exactly as it should be?

Looking around at the people filling my small apartment—the friends who chose to be there, who saw me, flaws and all—I realized that maybe life wasn't about achieving a perfect ideal. It was about accepting where I was, finding joy in small victories, and letting go of rigid expectations.

Ana caught my eye from across the room, her smile warm and knowing. For the first time in weeks, I felt a genuine smile spread across my face. Perhaps life's richness lay not in reaching predetermined milestones but in cherishing the people and moments that made the journey worthwhile.

As my younger brother blew out his candles, I felt a newfound freedom within me—a lightness as though the inner walls I had built were slowly crumbling, leaving me open to simply being.

ELDER ANASTASIA LOOKED at me, her gaze piercing yet compassionate. "The Sun," she said, gesturing to the card that lay on the table, "represents joy, vitality, and optimism when placed in the House of Children. It encourages you to balance the wonder of your inner child with the responsibilities of adulthood."

She leaned forward, her voice a gentle reminder. "You, Prince Aaron, are at a pivotal moment. You must learn to balance the duties that life demands of you with the curiosity and joy that once came so naturally. Embrace challenges not as burdens but as opportunities for growth."

Her words settled over me, and I found myself looking at the Sun card again. The child on the card radiated a sense of freedom I hadn't felt in years.

"Do you understand, Prince Aaron?"

"Yes," I replied. "The Sun in the House of Children reminds me that I don't have to abandon the joy and openness of my childhood. I can let these qualities guide me as I face adult challenges."

Elder Anastasia nodded, satisfaction gleaming in her eyes. "Take this wisdom forward. Let the light of the Sun illuminate both your path as a leader and your quest for truth. Balance and harmony are the true sources of your strength."

For a moment, I felt as if Elder Anastasia had not just read the cards but had seen directly into my soul. As I absorbed her words, I knew that my journey forward would be guided by both my inner child and my adult self, united in purpose and ready to face the world ahead.

Position 5 House of Work

Elder Anastasia sat at the dark oak table, her silver hair softly framing her face as her eyes flickered with insight. The long sleeves of her azure robe flowed as she reached over the cards spread before her.

"Who will assume Position Five, the House of Work?" she asked, her voice reverberating with quiet authority. "This role symbolizes our drive, our work ethic, and our resilience. It is the strength to rise above adversity and the endurance to persist through life's demands. The card that occupies this position will reveal insights into what propels you forward in the realm of worldly pursuits."

She closed her eyes briefly, then opened them with a clarity that made the room fall silent. As she drew a card, a figure stepped forward from the crowd.

"I, The Fool, shall take this place," he announced. The Fool was dressed in a vibrant Greek tunic, falling just above his knees, the colors vivid against his whimsical hat, which sported a pair of floppy donkey ears. A stick slung over his shoulder held a small, knotted bundle, and by his side pranced a lively little dog, snapping playfully at his belt bag. His carefree air brought a ripple of laughter through the crowd, but Elder Anastasia watched him closely.

"An unconventional choice," she observed. "Why would The Fool represent the House of Work?"

"Isn't all work a form of folly?" The Fool asked with a mischievous glint in his eyes. "We labor and toil, each step into the unknown, fueled by our dreams and ambitions. Isn't that, in itself, a sort of madness?"

A murmur swept through the grand hall as his words resonated. Elder Anastasia nodded thoughtfully.

"Your presence in this House brings a unique perspective. The Fool embodies beginnings, spontaneity, and resilience in the face of the unknown. You remind us that work isn't simply a pursuit of material gain; it's a journey, one of self-discovery and exploration."

I looked between Elder Anastasia and The Fool, their words stirring questions within me. Was my purpose in work solely to fulfill duties and meet expectations? Or was there something more—a quest for growth, an adventure on its own, right?

The room seemed to hold its breath, awaiting my response, but I knew these answers could not be given to me. They could only be lived.

SIERRA'S LIVING ROOM was a sanctuary, a calm oasis set apart from the world's relentless demands. The scent of vanilla incense wafted through the air, mingling with the warm aroma of freshly brewed herbal tea. A rustic coffee table sat between us, laden with mismatched cups and Sierra's tea set. The eclectic decor—woven rugs, colorful throw pillows, and framed photographs of Sierra's infectious smile—invited a sense of ease.

Sierra sat across from me, poised and radiant, her long black hair cascading over her shoulders and her dark eyes sharp with insight. I handed her my résumé, feeling the crinkle of the slightly rumpled pages.

"Would you mind looking this over for me?" I asked, trying to mask my nervousness.

"Of course, honey," she said, smiling as she scanned the pages. "You've held quite a few roles, I see. But if I may offer some advice, try condensing this down to one page, highlighting your most relevant positions."

"I know," I admitted. "I've taken on so many jobs over the years that it's hard to know what to include. But nothing really lasted—only two roles over a year."

She looked up, her gaze direct. "It's important to create a stable employment history. Did you leave all of these voluntarily?"

"Yes," I replied, exhaling. "Every time, it just got to be too much. I didn't feel I could ask for help, so I quit."

Sierra took a deep breath, her gaze softening. "Honey, you need to work on handling your anxiety. This habit of quitting when things get hard is holding you back."

I nodded, feeling the weight of her words. "I know. I've risen to manage accounts and even became a Director of Operations at one point. But each time, the pressures became too much—unsupportive coworkers and unresponsive bosses. I couldn't take it."

"Perfectionism is a double-edged sword," she said, setting the résumé down and leaning toward me. "You're not just striving for excellence; you're holding yourself to an impossible standard, afraid of imperfection. But growth comes through persistence, not perfection. Embrace your mistakes—they're part of the journey."

Her words settled deeply within me, challenging the beliefs I'd carried for so long. I took the résumé back, her advice echoing in my mind.

"Revise this," she encouraged. "Not just as a list of jobs, but as a testament to your resilience. Let it tell a story, not of roles abandoned, but of lessons learned."

THE ROOM HAD GROWN so quiet that the candle flames seemed to have their own voice, crackling softly in the stillness. Elder Anastasia sat like a sentinel behind the oak table, her face cast in shadow. The Fool perched on a stool nearby, his donkey-eared hat giving him an air of jest, but his eyes were earnest.

"Your life has followed a winding path, undefined and limitless," The Fool began. "This lack of structure can cause panic. Without constraints or rules, we're adrift, uncertain of where we're going. You must find balance."

"What do you mean?" I asked, searching for clarity. "Are you saying that my future in the House of Work is both an open journey and a potential burden?"

The Fool leaned back, considering. "Indeed, Prince Aaron. The journey is filled with both wonder and fear. Yes, your work is an adventure, a journey, but without a destination, it's easy to get lost."

"So, I need to balance freedom with structure," I said, understanding dawning. "To honor the journey while setting goals along the way."

"Precisely." Elder Anastasia's voice was steady, filled with approval. "The Fool reminds us that each step is both an end and a beginning. Seek adventure, yes, but remember to ground yourself with purpose and direction."

The Fool grinned, tipping his hat playfully. "Without grounding, your journey may lack meaning. You'll always be searching but never finding."

I took a deep breath, feeling as if another piece of life's puzzle had fallen into place.

"Thank you both," I said, my voice filled with gratitude. "For reminding me that my work is both a quest and a means of building something real."

The Fool winked, his eyes bright with mischief, while Elder Anastasia nodded, a smile of deep satisfaction on her face. I left with a renewed sense of purpose, understanding that my journey in work was as much about discovery as it was about achievement and that each step was building the foundation of who I was meant to become.

Position 6 House Of Love

"Who will take the sixth position, the House of Love?" Elder Anastasia intoned, her voice carrying a subtle weight that rippled through the room.

A quiet rustling from a nearby tapestry caught my attention. It depicted the Garden of Eden, its woven figures seeming to stir within their fabric confines. My pulse quickened as the forms detached themselves from the tapestry, stepping into the room as if crossing the boundary between myth and reality.

"We, the Lovers, will assume the role of the House of Love," they declared in harmonious unison. They stood side by side, draped in fig leaves—the man held an apple aloft, embodying temptation and forbidden knowledge, and the woman carried an albino snake coiled around her arm, symbolizing both wisdom and deceit.

"Love," they continued, "is our realm, encompassing both truth and malevolence."

Elder Anastasia observed them with intrigue. "Ah, the Lovers—a fitting representation. Would you share how your presence here illuminates Prince Aaron's House of Love?"

The male figure lifted the apple toward the light, its surface glinting as it caught the flickering glow of candles. "Love is like this apple, Prince Aaron—rich and fulfilling, yet it bears seeds of discord. In your quest for love, have you considered the cost of your choices and the responsibilities they carry?"

Before I could respond, the woman extended her arm, the snake unfurling itself as she began to speak. "In love, as in life, duality is inescapable," she said. "I carry the snake, a symbol of wisdom but also of malice. Love may lead you to enlightenment or entanglement. The path you take depends on your discernment. How will you navigate this duality?"

Their words pierced me, exposing the complex nature of my affections—the beauty and the darkness, the intimacy and the tension that defined love itself.

THE MORNING SUN FILTERED through the drapes, casting a warm glow over the room. Patrick stood before me, his height imposing, his blue eyes blazing. His blond hair was meticulously combed, an image of control.

"Do you love me?" he asked, his tone chilling.

I held his gaze, refusing to answer. His fist struck my gut, and pain exploded through my abdomen. "When I wake up, my coffee and breakfast better be on the table. And make sure it's hot," he demanded, punctuating his words with a sharp punch to my face.

I stumbled backward, but he caught me, pulling me into an iron embrace. His hug was tight, almost suffocating, as if he were trying to bind me to him permanently. "Your love for me," he whispered, his voice soft but laden with menace, "is more than I ever hoped for."

At that moment, I felt our love's paradox—intense yet terrifying, beautiful yet brutal. Caught between his fists and his silence, I realized the painful complexity of our connection. As I lay there, his voice echoing in my ears, I managed to whisper, "I love you, too, Patrick."

His hand met my face with such force that my world spun before I hit the cold, unforgiving ceramic tiles. Sharp pain radiated through my nose, and I lay still, collecting myself as darkness clouded the edges of my vision.

LATER THAT EVENING, the door creaked open. Ramona, my friend and roommate, stood in the doorway, her expression shifting from shock to concern. Her presence, always warm and grounded, filled the room with a familiar jasmine scent, calming me.

"What happened?" she asked, crossing the room and crouching beside me.

I forced a casual tone. "Nothing, I just fell."

She gave me a look of disbelief, extending her hand to help me up. She knew me too well to believe my feeble excuse, but she didn't press. Instead, she led me to the kitchen counter, her hand firm on my shoulder. We began cooking together, falling into our practiced rhythm. Ramona worked alongside me silently, and there was a quiet understanding between us as we chopped vegetables and stirred pots.

The kitchen was filled with the comforting aroma of garlic and onions sizzling in olive oil. Outside, the sun dipped lower, casting the room in warm, golden hues. In that small space, we found a shared comfort, each tending to the people in our lives with unspoken loyalty.

<hr />

DARNELL AND PATRICK entered the dining room, taking their seats at the polished mahogany table. Ramona settled into Darnell's lap, their familiar ease evident in the way they exchanged a private smile. I placed a steak before Patrick carefully arranged it just the way he liked it.

But he glanced at the plate with mild disdain. "I wanted chicken, not steak."

Swallowing my frustration, I returned to the kitchen to cook chicken. Minutes later, I set the new plate before Patrick. He pushed it aside. "On second thought, I'd prefer fish."

I returned to the kitchen yet again, rummaging through the refrigerator only to find that we were out of fresh fish. "The only option we have is frozen fish sticks," I told him.

"No, I don't want those," he replied dismissively. "Actually, let's just go out."

Frustration bubbled up, but before I could respond, Patrick picked up the original steak I had prepared and began eating it. Then he motioned for me to join him, pulling me onto his lap as he continued eating, savoring each bite. It was as if he had planned it all, as if this display of control was his real meal. I sat there, feeling the weight of his whims trapped in his grasp.

<hr />

AS THE EVENING SETTLED into a comfortable rhythm, Maria joined Ramona and me at the table. The three of us sipped wine and shared laughter, relishing the simple joy of companionship. The night stretched on, the quiet intimacy of our conversation filling the room.

Darnell, Ramona's husband, appeared in the doorway, signaling with a gentle look that it was time for her to join him. She squeezed our hands, excusing herself with a smile that spoke of shared understanding.

Patrick soon followed, casting a look that drew me to him. I excused myself, feeling the complex pull of duty and desire as I followed him toward our room. These moments—quiet, intimate, and tinged with unspoken promises—were the fragile pieces that made up my life.

THE LOVERS REAPPEARED, their forms ethereal as they emerged from the mist of Elder Anastasia's incense. Their fig leaves and symbolic emblems—the apple and the snake—embodied the duality of love and choice.

The male figure spoke, his voice smooth yet commanding. "Change is essential, Prince Aaron, but it must come gradually. To resist change is to wither, but to embrace it is to thrive."

The female figure continued, her voice like warm sunlight filtering through a forest canopy. "Release old habits and beliefs that no longer serve you. Cast off doubt and fear. Only by shedding the past can you make space for new growth."

The male figure resumed, his gaze steady. "Healing is a journey, not a moment. It requires patience and endurance. You will face challenges, but resilience will guide you through."

The woman added, "Balance is key. As you shift, maintain harmony within yourself. Only by balancing old and new can you truly flourish."

Their voices merged in perfect harmony. "In love, discern carefully. True love supports and elevates. Anything less is a shadow, an illusion that will bind you in sorrow."

Their message resonated deeply, leaving me with a profound sense of both clarity and unease. As they faded back into the tapestry, their advice lingered in the incense-laden air—a guide for navigating the complexities of love and transformation.

I looked to Elder Anastasia, seeking her insight. She nodded, her expression serene but knowing. "The cards reveal what is true, not what is easy. You stand at a crossroads, Prince Aaron, where love holds the potential to build or destroy. What you do with this wisdom is yours to decide."

As the session continued, my thoughts drifted back to the Lovers, their dual symbols of the apple and the snake. They were a reminder of love's power to elevate or entangle. And I pondered, with both hope and trepidation, the paths that lay before me.

Position 7 House of Family

"Who shall claim the seventh position, House of Family?" Elder Anastasia's voice carried a soft reverence, her gaze lifting momentarily toward the heavens. "The House of Family delves into inner emotions, the sanctuary of one's heart, and the haven of spirituality. It is where one seeks solace in times of distress."

Her words struck a deep chord within me, bringing to mind my father—the stern yet benevolent king—and my siblings, each wrestling with their own destinies.

A figure appeared, shimmering with an ethereal glow that seemed to defy the laws of time and space. It was The Tower, an embodiment of both power and transformation. His hair shifted colors like the northern lights, his skin luminous alabaster, and his gaze fixed with an intensity that pierced through the room's grandeur.

"I, The Tower, shall unveil the tapestry of this young man's familial journey," he declared, his voice reverberating through the grand hall. He turned toward Ximena, my sister, his eyes softening as he took in her presence.

"Ximena, lone sister among three brothers—each a flame in their own right," he said, his words weaving a vivid image of her strength and grace. "At sixteen, you sensed the path that destiny was weaving for you."

Ximena's voice, calm but fierce, broke through the silence. "I've always felt part of something larger, a purpose beyond the immediate bonds of family."

The Tower nodded, acknowledging her intuition. "Indeed, family is a pilgrimage, an intricate design where each thread—the joys, sorrows, triumphs, and defeats—creates the grand tapestry of shared existence."

He shifted his gaze to me. "Prince Aaron, consider Ximena's insight. Family is not merely a sanctuary but a universe unto itself. Each member is a celestial body, held together by the invisible forces of love, destiny, and shared history."

As I looked at Ximena, a new appreciation dawned on me for the bonds that defined us—not merely as siblings but as woven strands in a greater design. Yet, beneath this moment of unity, a tension simmered.

Ximena's gaze grew somber as she addressed me. "Aaron, the mantle of caring for our mother now rests with you. It is your duty to guard her peace, as she once cared for you."

Her words felt heavy, almost accusing, as though she had already accepted a burden I had yet to shoulder fully.

"You stand as a naive idealist," she continued, her tone sharp. "Do you truly believe we'll rally to your side? Each of us faces our own lives and our own struggles. You can't ask us to bear this weight with you."

Santino, our youngest brother, leaned against a marble pillar, a subtle smirk tugging at his lips. "Ximena's right," he murmured, crossing his arms. "We have our own burdens to carry, Aaron. Why should yours fall on us as well?"

I felt their words sinking in like stones. "Is this truly how you both feel?" I asked, my voice barely concealing my disappointment. "Mother has been the thread binding our family together. Is it not our collective responsibility to ensure her final years are peaceful?"

Santino scoffed, his expression hardening. "Idealism is a luxury. Reality demands sacrifices, and we all have our limits."

Ximena softened, but her resolve remained. "It's not about love or respect, Aaron. It's the hard truth that each of us is tethered to our own obligations. You can't demand a sacrifice we're not able to give."

The weight of their words settled around me like a dense fog, but The Tower's gaze returned to me, piercing through the haze.

"Prince Aaron," he said, his tone both gentle and firm, "the labyrinth of family obligations is winding and treacherous. Yet it is within these trials that we find love's true depth and purpose. Whatever path you choose, know it is but one thread in the larger tapestry of your life's journey."

I looked from Ximena to Santino, then back at The Tower, realizing that, though I stood at a crossroads, the journey was mine alone to navigate.

I ventured to speak, my voice uncertain. "The Tower often signifies chaos and disruption. Am I to expect that family, too, will be a proving ground?"

The Tower's eyes glimmered with a strange warmth. "Young Prince, chaos is not your undoing but your teacher. Life's storms—especially those within a family—forge resilience and reveal the core of who you are. They strip away illusions, leaving only what is true."

Elder Anastasia's voice filled the silence. "You have endured storms, Prince Aaron, and they have shaped you. Betrayals, misunderstandings, and losses—these shadows have fortified your spirit."

She turned another card, revealing The Sun. "Even after the darkest tempests, the Sun returns. You are stronger now, a warrior tempered by trials, not a mere survivor."

My heart swelled at her words. I looked at the cards before me: The Tower, The Sun, and finally, The Fool, representing renewal and courage.

The Tower spoke again. "I am not ruin, but rebirth. I am change, swift, and often brutal. The storms I bring dismantle the old, but they also lay foundations for the new."

"You are both adversary and teacher," I whispered, beginning to grasp his meaning.

"Precisely," he replied. "Your trials within the family, the upheavals you face—they tear down old structures to make way for something stronger. In family, as in life, these upheavals are the lessons that reveal your truest self."

Elder Anastasia nodded approvingly, her gaze filled with both compassion and respect. "Take this wisdom with you, Prince Aaron. Every ending brought by The Tower is a prelude to a new beginning. You will emerge not as a ruin but as a fortress rebuilt, stronger and wiser."

Understanding washed over me. "I see now. The Tower is not to be feared, but to be met with courage—as an opportunity for growth."

The Tower shimmered, his form contracting into the image on his card, leaving me with a strange sense of calm and purpose. The mantle of family was not a burden to be resented nor a duty to be avoided. It was a journey, a proving ground, and a gift.

With one last glance at the cards—The Tower, The Sun, The Fool—I felt ready to embrace whatever lay ahead, knowing that each storm would reveal a new layer of strength and clarity within me.

Position 8 House of Magic

Elder Anastasia's gaze shifted to the Tarot cards before her, a quiet anticipation evident in her eyes. She lifted her head, her voice almost a whisper, yet it filled the room.

"Who shall assume the eighth position, the House of Magic? This house is known for its allure and its challenge, shattering conventional boundaries to offer a new view of reality."

With a steady hand, she turned over a card. Intricate symbols danced across it, their meaning elusive yet enticing.

"This house," she explained, fingers grazing the ornate patterns, "represents encounters with those who defy explanation, who exist beyond the known. You may feel unsteady, perhaps even unsettled. But embrace these moments, Prince Aaron. The unknown is a teacher, not an adversary. Each experience will reveal a deeper wisdom."

"I've always respected the mystical arts," I said. "But the council views them as frivolous, even foolish."

Elder Anastasia chuckled softly. "That is the lesson. The House of Magic lives in balance between intuition and reason. Your council may learn to appreciate what they dismiss today, just as you may." She pointed a slender finger at me. "You will be their guiding light."

At that moment, another figure emerged—a man with dark, curly hair pulled back, dressed simply in faded jeans. He bore no crown or robe, yet his presence was magnetic.

"I am Merlin the Magician," he announced, his voice a melodic command.

With a wave of his hand, a silver light formed around his right palm, flowing up his arm like molten metal. His left hand moved in tandem, conjuring a different energy—a prismatic arc that flickered with chaotic beauty, stretching toward me as if alive, as if curious.

"What is this?" I asked, unable to look away.

"This is the duality of your path, Prince Aaron," Merlin said. "The white luminescence is purity and wisdom, the knowledge you seek. The prismatic arc represents choices, challenges, and the countless experiences that will shape you. Together, they will guide and refine you."

"They're directed toward me?"

Merlin nodded. "You are the axis, the point at which these forces converge. Your choices will shape their energy and, in turn, shape you."

The energies swirled around me, vibrant and dynamic. A sense of peace settled over me as I realized that this journey—filled with the unknown—was mine to take. For the first time, I felt ready to embrace it fully.

※

THE BAR WAS AWASH IN amber light, the walls lined with worn photographs and old newspaper clippings. The hum of smooth jazz filled the air, and each table held its own private story. I had come seeking refuge from family turmoil, hoping to find some peace in the dimly lit solitude.

Beside me sat Maria, my confidante, who knew when to speak and when to simply be. I was lost in thought when a stranger approached.

"Good evening, handsome. Might I have the honor of your name?" His voice was warm and inviting, carrying an air of ease.

I looked up. He was tall and well-built, with dark hair neatly styled and eyes that were a deep, comforting brown. His expression was open, his smile genuine.

"Aaron," I replied. "And you, sir?"

"Daren," he said, extending his hand. "These are my friends. We're traveling from Los Angeles to New Orleans for Halloween."

As I shook his hand, I noticed a spark of excitement in his eyes. His friends seemed equally welcoming, as if this meeting were as natural as breathing. Another of his friends, Jacob, offered his hand.

"Nice to meet you, Aaron. I was going to be on this trip, but I have a reason to stay," Jacob said with a slight smile, nodding at someone across the room.

"So you're offering your ticket to me?" I asked, caught between intrigue and disbelief.

Jacob laughed. "Life is full of unexpected invitations. Maybe you need this more than I do."

Daren leaned closer, his gaze sincere. "Sometimes, a spontaneous detour is just what we need to realign our lives. You seem like a man who could use a change of scenery."

I glanced at Maria, who gave an encouraging nod. I could feel the weight of family drama and past choices pressing down on me, and here was a chance—an escape, an adventure.

"Why not?" I said finally, a slow smile forming. "Perhaps it's time I embraced a little spontaneity."

Laughter and cheers erupted from the group. Daren's eyes sparkled as he looked at me, his smile widening.

"Aaron," he said in a low voice as he leaned in, "you know when someone's intentions are genuine. Trust that, and let's enjoy this moment. Tonight, let's forget the obligations that weigh you down and simply live."

Our hands brushed, and an unspoken connection passed between us—a shared understanding, a promise. We spent the evening talking, laughing, and exploring the bar as if it were a hidden world. When the night deepened, he led me outside, where the cool air and the city's lights wrapped around us, promising freedom.

The next morning, I felt a quiet resolve. Life, with all its unpredictability, lay ahead, and for once, I was ready to embrace it without reservation.

MERLIN APPEARED BEFORE me again, his form solid yet shimmering, as if composed of light and shadow. His gaze met mine with knowing intensity.

"You have danced on the edge of greatness only to step back," he said, his voice a quiet echo in the chamber.

He raised his hands, and the same energies appeared—white light in his right hand, a prismatic arc in his left. They swirled together, vibrant and alive, reaching out to encircle me.

"Draw strength from these experiences. Let them feed your creativity," Merlin continued. "Remember, every choice you make shapes the path ahead."

As Merlin's form faded into the shadows, the weight of his words settled over me. I felt a profound sense of alignment, as if each experience had indeed led me here, preparing me for the road I was destined to travel. The House of

Magic had opened my eyes, and I was ready to step forward, leaving the past behind as I embraced the boundless unknown.

Position 9 House of Apprenticeship

Elder Anastasia, keeper of the ancient tarot, sat with her hands trembling but steady as she shuffled a deck of cards as worn as the tomes lining the chamber walls. Each card was a hand-painted masterpiece, embodying archetypes that had guided both princes and paupers through their paths in life.

"Who shall claim the ninth position in the House of Apprenticeship?" she asked, her voice resonant with the wisdom of ages. "This house embodies one's capacity for learning, thirst for experience, and unique strengths."

As she paused, an elderly man stepped forward, his presence dignified and timeless.

"I, The Hermit, shall occupy the House of Apprenticeship," he declared. His voice was soft yet carried through the room like a whispering wind, each word seeming to echo with ancient knowledge.

The Hermit's cloak shimmered like stardust, woven from strands of silver and moonlight, cascading down his form in a luminous flow. His hood obscured his face, save for the wisp of a white beard that hinted at a life steeped in wisdom. In his left hand, he held a scepter, an exquisite fusion of crystal and wood, as if drawn from the earth and sky alike.

As he approached, he extended his bony hand and bestowed the scepter upon me. The moment our fingers touched, a surge of energy jolted through me, a spark of understanding.

"I represent your authentic self and the aspirations you hold dear," he spoke, his tone imbued with sincerity. "My quest is one of integrity, and in you, I sense a similar yearning—a path where truth is a guiding light."

I bowed my head. "Your words honor me," I replied, my voice quiet and respectful. "But why do you, the Hermit, represent the House of Apprenticeship? Shouldn't you belong to a realm of mastery?"

A soft smile tugged at the corners of his mouth. "Wisdom is a journey without end. Even mastery holds within it the heart of a student, for a true master is ever learning, ever seeking."

Elder Anastasia nodded, her eyes glimmering. "Indeed, wisdom lies within wisdom itself."

"Precisely," The Hermit agreed, his gaze shifting back to me. "In this quest for understanding, you, Prince Aaron, are a perpetual apprentice, led not by the urge for completion but by a thirst for depth. This scepter symbolizes your path, a quest that is never fully complete."

With a gentle nod, he withdrew, his cloak trailing behind him like a river of stars. Elder Anastasia's gaze met mine. "Remember, Prince Aaron, the cards offer guidance, but it is you who must tread the path they illuminate."

In that sacred chamber, I understood this journey was mine alone to walk, though I would be joined by archetypes and energies that would guide me through each twist and turn.

THE ATMOSPHERE OF MY childhood home was a stark contrast—my mother's warmth and encouragement were light. At the same time, my father's disapproval cast shadows that darkened my dreams. As a young adult, the word "cosmetology" would fill me with excitement, conjuring visions of a vibrant salon, the hum of happy clients, and the fragrance of beauty products.

At twenty, I dreamed of becoming a cosmetologist, standing at a polished counter, brushes and palettes neatly arrayed. But my father had other plans. The day I received a withdrawal notice from cosmetology school—something he had arranged behind my back—my dreams were upended. In their place, he handed me an enrollment form for a receptionist program.

"See? A real job with a real future," he insisted.

"But it's not my future," I muttered under my breath.

Though he openly disparaged education, he had co-signed a student loan for this "practical" path. He arranged my commute as if plotting every detail of a life I hadn't chosen. In secret, I enrolled in a bartending course—not exactly a grand rebellion, but it brought me joy. Still, had he known, his fury would have been swift. For him, any education beyond basic employment was frivolous, a waste.

"Why bother with more schooling? It's pointless. No diploma will change a thing," he would often say, his words slicing through my confidence like a corrosive acid.

My mother, by contrast, encouraged my creative pursuits, especially in the kitchen. She was the first to taste my cookies and cakes, offering unreserved praise for my culinary experiments. But my father's critiques loomed like storm clouds, casting shadows over even my small triumphs. If the crust was too dark, he'd scoff, "Burnt, can't you get it right?" If it was too light, he'd mutter, "Undercooked, you need to try harder." Slowly, the kitchen, my sanctuary, began to feel more like a battleground, each recipe a skirmish in the endless war for validation.

Every critique, every disapproving look, eroded my confidence, turning my dreams into distant echoes. My father's voice was more than just sound—it was an oppressive presence, a shadow cast over every ambition.

In a house divided, where my mother's encouragement clashed with my father's disapproval, I found myself standing at a crossroads. I wondered if I could ever break free to chase the light while leaving his shadow behind.

THE HERMIT'S VOICE pulled me back to the present, steady and unwavering. "Endurance in life's lessons and in work is essential," he began. "Life is a maze with countless twists. Naysayers will emerge, both from the outside and from within, taking the form of doubt and fear. The key to navigating this maze is self-knowledge."

"Don't let one person's views define your life," said a voice that seemed to come from nowhere.

Startled, I looked around. "Who spoke?"

Elder Anastasia leaned closer. "A reminder from the spirit world. You are not alone on this journey."

The Hermit nodded. "Let no one else's limits become the boundary of your dreams. You, and you alone, hold the power to shape your destiny." His staff, gleaming with an otherworldly light, seemed to bridge earth and sky, grounding his words in something larger than life. "Your father is but a chapter in the story of your life. Let him be a part, not the conclusion. Write the ending yourself—one that honors your aspirations, not his criticisms."

His words felt like a beacon dispelling years of doubt and hesitation, lifting a weight I hadn't realized I carried.

"Endurance isn't just survival," he continued. "It is thriving amid adversity, turning resistance into fuel. Use it to build, not just endure."

I felt a rush of clarity, as though the murkiness that had clouded my path was lifting. Elder Anastasia met my gaze. "Your journey is your own, Prince Aaron, and only you can see it through."

The Hermit's form began to fade, his cloak trailing like a cascade of stardust as he returned to the shadows. I stood there, feeling the strength of his words settle within me.

For the first time, I felt ready to reclaim my path and rewrite my story in the ink of my own dreams.

Position 10 House of Mental State

I stood in the grand hall, surrounded by an energy that seemed to pulse from the semi-precious stones, talismans, and the presence of the Tarot characters who had already assumed their roles in this divine theater. The air was charged with anticipation.

"Who will take the tenth position, the House of Mental State?" Elder Anastasia's voice broke the silence. "This House represents one's inner mind and mental state, the way we perceive ourselves and are perceived by others, and how we respond to life's challenges."

A figure in rich red robes stepped forward—an elderly man with a voice as resonant as a cathedral bell and as soothing as a hymn.

"I, the Pope, shall assume the role of the House of Mental State." He looked directly at me, his robe glowing in the candlelight, his triple crown amplifying the room's warm glow.

"I symbolize the wisdom of ages and the lens through which you view your mental landscape. Prince Aaron, do you find yourself navigating the corridors of your mind through the compass of ancestral wisdom? Or are you forging your own path?"

His question lingered in the air, and I felt a stirring within. The Pope's presence embodied the tension between tradition and personal insight—a tension I had not fully acknowledged until now.

WE SAT IN THE FAMILY lounge, a sanctuary of rich fabrics, handwoven rugs, and antique furniture, like silent witnesses to decades of family history. A golden chandelier cast a soft glow, and classical music hummed from an old record player as if my mother were trying to create a cocoon to escape reality.

Across from me, my mother held her teacup with the grace of a figure in a portrait, her serenity a stark contrast to the inner turbulence I was wrestling with.

"Aaron, they mean well," she said, setting her cup down with a gentle clink.

"But what if I choose my own partner? The future is uncertain—just as you and Father might still find a way back to each other."

"Let go of such notions," she replied, her voice firm. "That chapter is closed."

"You say that," I pressed, "but part of me feels you haven't truly let go. I think you'd sacrifice everything for Father again if given the chance."

She turned the conversation as she often did. "Are you still taking your medication?"

"Mother, why do we need to shift the subject to pills?" I replied, half-jokingly but with a seriousness she couldn't miss.

"You don't need them. A healer in Mexico could cure you in a heartbeat," she countered, deflecting my concerns with talk of supernatural remedies.

"A 'chicken-wielding healer' won't fix me, Mother. You even acknowledged I struggled in my youth!"

"You were just sensitive, a bit troubled," she replied, her gaze distant.

"Mother, I can't even recall most of my childhood," I said, leaning forward, the weight of my memories pressing down. "Can't we face that, at least? We've avoided these discussions for too long."

She looked at me, her eyes narrowing as if trying to see past the years. "What's troubling you, Aaron?"

"I'm thirty-five years old, and I still can't sleep properly. I have anxiety attacks and anger issues that don't feel normal. Don't you remember all the doctors, the endless tests, the appointments with psychologists?"

She sighed, brushing it off. "You're dramatic—just like your father."

"Mother, this isn't just drama. You sought all those consultations because you knew something was wrong."

She finally met my gaze before looking away, focusing on the intricate tablecloth. "Those were precautions. Every mother worries."

"When medicine didn't have answers, you went to mystics, curanderas, promises to saints like business contracts. What good has it done? We need to accept there's been a deeper issue all along. Can we finally acknowledge that?"

She looked away, eyes misting. "And what do you propose we do, Aaron? Dig into the past for answers that don't exist?"

"No, Mother. I want us to confront the past because it does hold answers—answers rooted in acceptance, not in denial."

She sat back, her shoulders sinking as if conceding. "Then let's search for your peace, even if it means facing the uncomfortable truths."

The room exhaled with us, the weight of years spent in avoidance finally lifting, if only slightly. For the first time, I felt a glimmer of hope that we might turn the page, leaving behind years of half-truths and silence.

BACK IN THE GRAND HALL, I felt the significance of the Pope's role more deeply.

"I have often sought guidance from ancestral teachings, but I also see tradition as a double-edged sword. It can guide us, but it can also confine us."

The Pope nodded. "A keen observation. Tradition offers us a foundation, but it is up to each individual to determine what they build upon it."

As he merged back with the other tarot figures, it felt as if the House of Mental State was more than a mirror of my inner world. It was a call to venture into the uncharted corridors of my mind and emerge with a blend of inherited wisdom and my own truths.

Position 11 House of Friends in Life

Elder Anastasia, cloaked in robes adorned with astrological symbols, shuffled the tarot cards with an elegance that felt both earthly and otherworldly. The air hummed as she spoke, her voice melodious and rich with purpose.

"Who will take their place in the House of Friends in Life?" she asked, her voice resonating through the chamber.

The card she flipped was The World. As she laid it on the table, the room transformed, expanding to feel boundless, where the physical and the ethereal seemed to blur. A young man materialized, carved from pure vitality. His eyes held an intensity tempered by kindness, and his muscular frame carried an orb representing the world on his shoulders—a weight that seemed to energize rather than burden him.

He approached with steady, purposeful strides. As he neared, the orb he carried began to shrink as though an invisible force molded it to fit perfectly into his open palm. Extending it toward me, he spoke, his voice powerful yet calm.

"I am The World," he said. "The world is now within your grasp. Shape it as you will, but remember—only through balance and love can you truly transform it."

The message resonated deep within as if he were handing me not just the world but also the responsibility to honor and care for it. Elder Anastasia looked at me with a gentle yet profound expression.

"The World card in the House of Friends in Life," she explained, "reminds you that your friends, from childhood and beyond, play a crucial role in shaping your world. They are both your anchor and your horizon. Nurture these connections with love and respect; they are co-creators in the world you wish to manifest."

AUNT DOLORES' DRAWING room was a sanctuary of calm, far removed from the chaotic rhythms of my daily life. The rich hues of the mahogany furniture, the softness of the oriental rug, and the meticulously chosen art pieces created a serene balance, offering a space for reflection. The air was tinged with the fragrance of fresh flowers and aged leather—a scent that sharpened the senses and softened the heart.

Seated in her favorite armchair, Aunt Dolores, with her fiery red hair blazing in the sunlight streaming through the lace curtains, looked every bit like a portrait. She held her teacup with a gentle grace, each sip as deliberate as her words.

"Tell me about your friends, Aaron," she asked, her tone both inquisitive and understanding.

I hesitated, then spoke, trying to navigate the complexity of these relationships. "There's Ana. She's been in my life for a decade now."

"Is she a true friend?" Aunt Dolores asked, her gaze steady. "Or merely a companion by circumstance, someone you converse with out of habit rather than need?"

I considered this. "With Ana, there's no need for reciprocity. We listen to each other without expecting anything in return."

Aunt Dolores set her teacup down, a thoughtful look on her face. "And what about those who go out of their way for you?"

"Collin, for example. He helps me with medical appointments and always makes time to check in on me. Our support is mutual."

Aunt Dolores nodded. "And can you distinguish between these types of friendships?"

"Collin genuinely cares for my well-being. Ana, on the other hand, is someone I talk to because I feel compelled to be useful, even though she doesn't necessarily reciprocate."

She raised an eyebrow. "Does this pattern also apply to your family? Do they hold your trust?"

I took a deep breath. "My family's trustworthiness is complicated, especially with my father."

"What lies behind this distrust?" she asked gently.

"They've never given me a reason to fully trust them, but I don't completely distrust them either. I confide in Ana more than I do in my family, even though I know Ana could betray me."

Her eyes softened. "That doesn't sound like a true friendship," she said, her words touching on an uncomfortable truth.

The room seemed to close in, the atmosphere growing heavier as if echoing the weight of her words. The afternoon light was fading, casting long shadows, and the scent of Earl Grey tea mingled with the smell of the old leather-bound books lining the walls.

"It's how I was raised. My father ingrained in me that family couldn't be trusted," I admitted. "I internalized his perspective."

Aunt Dolores adjusted the folds of her dress, the light from a nearby Tiffany lamp casting rainbows across the fabric. "Family can be a foundation, but it doesn't have to be your only one. If your immediate family isn't a source of trust, it's natural to build a new family of friends who can be."

Her gaze held mine, steady and unwavering. "Why do you distrust your family so deeply?"

The room fell silent, the only sound the faint ticking of the grandfather clock. "They don't understand me," I finally said. "I'm gay, and I struggle with mental health issues. They either avoid these topics or dismiss them. How can I talk openly with people who can't—or won't—understand?"

She closed her eyes, a look of empathy crossing her face. "Sometimes, family isn't the one we're born into but the one we create. You need a circle that values who you are, not who they want you to be."

As I rose to leave, a shift occurred within me, subtle yet profound. Aunt Dolores' words lingered, transforming the way I viewed friendship. My friends were not merely a support system; they were active participants in shaping the life I aspired to build. They were my chosen family. Stepping out into the warm embrace of the setting sun, I felt lighter, as if a burden had been lifted from my shoulders.

BACK IN THE GRAND HALL, I reflected on the messages I had received from Aunt Dolores and The World card. As if hearing my thoughts, The World spoke again, its form shifting like a living tapestry.

"The wisdom of Aunt Dolores is etched within you, young Prince Aaron," it said. "Her insights resonate with the very fibers of your being. Don't take her words lightly; they align with cosmic truths that will guide you."

"Aunt Dolores spoke to me about balancing kindness and strength, about knowing when to trust and when to build my own path."

The World nodded, the orb in its hand shimmering. "Each piece of wisdom is a key, Aaron. Each key unlocks doors to growth, conflict, peace, or love. You may not yet know which door each key will open, but the keys themselves are valuable. Guard them well."

"I will remember that," I said.

"Remembering is only the beginning. Living with intention, treating each step as both your first and last—that is how you embody The World's wisdom."

The counsel from Aunt Dolores, now illuminated by The World's guidance, had woven a tapestry of understanding within me, equipping me for the journey that lay ahead.

Position 12 House of Enemies

The grand hall, with its deep purple tapestries adorned in intricate silver filigree, felt like it existed between realms. Glowing orbs floated near the ceiling, casting a soft, ethereal light that made the room seem otherworldly—a sanctuary removed from the weight of my daily responsibilities. The scent of incense hung heavy, creating an atmosphere that blurred the line between reality and the mystical.

As I sat immersed in the room's aura, a sudden tremor shook the foundation. The tapestries whipped violently as though a fierce storm had swept through the space. When the tremors ceased, silence fell, and the center of the room remained vacant—no tarot figure had yet claimed the position of the House of Enemies.

Elder Anastasia's eyes flickered with unease. "Is there anyone who will assume this position?" Her voice held an unusual note of urgency.

The silence deepened as those who had already claimed their roles glanced at each other, hesitant. I turned to Elder Anastasia, the air thick with uncertainty.

"What happens if this position remains unclaimed, Elder Anastasia?" I asked, feeling a sense of dread creeping in.

She sighed, her gaze heavy. "It is rare, Prince Aaron. The House of Enemies represents both the external challenges you will face and the inner adversities that lie within. If no character steps forward, it may signify that your greatest adversities are elusive—unpredictable, hidden, or perhaps even within yourself."

Just as her words settled, a shadowed figure began to emerge from the room's dim corner. Cloaked in a mist tinged with deep crimson, she moved gracefully to the center of the room.

"The role of the House of Enemies will be fulfilled," Elder Anastasia said, her voice barely above a whisper. "May we all be prepared for what lies ahead."

The figure stepped fully into the light, revealing herself as The Queen of Cups. Her presence was serene yet powerful, cloaked in flowing azure robes that shimmered like water and celestial patterns that cascaded over her. A crown of sapphire and aquamarine rested upon her twilight-colored hair, which fell in loose waves down her back. In her hands, she held two chalices filled with a mysterious liquid that seemed to catch and reflect the light as if it were made of liquid stardust.

"I am the Queen of Cups," she announced, her voice soft yet resonant. "Though it may seem strange, I am here to guide Prince Aaron in his House of Enemies. For his greatest adversaries are not strangers or distant foes, but the complexities within his own family and the shadows of his own mind."

Her words pierced through me, resonating with memories I had long buried. My greatest struggles were not battles fought on open fields. Still, silent wars are waged within the confines of family bonds and inner turmoil.

"Prince Aaron," the Queen continued, "your fears are not of others but are rooted in the very relationships closest to you. To assume this mantle is to walk a path that could either lead to healing or plunge you deeper into the labyrinth of your own heart."

The room was silent, each character, each presence seeming to hold their breath as her words settled over me.

"Elder Anastasia, we must proceed with this reading," the Count interjected, his tone urgent. "We cannot leave Prince Aaron without answers."

The Gypsy Queen stepped forward. "Then let us ask him directly," she suggested, her gaze piercing.

"Prince Aaron," she said, her tone both gentle and commanding, "do you remember your true identity?"

"I recall fragments," I replied cautiously. "Moments, faces, feelings... but a clear sense of self still eludes me. I feel as if I am caught between dreams and reality."

"It's a blockade he has imposed upon himself," said the Seer, her tone resolute. "A wall of his own making, perhaps born of a wound too painful to confront directly."

A voice of dissent emerged. "You led Aaron astray with your interpretation," Ximena retorted, her gaze directed at the Seer, her tone edged with accusation.

Justice stepped forward to settle the dispute.

"This reading was the Seer's task," he said, his voice carrying a weight that silenced the room. "The responsibility of the interpretation rests upon her alone, and now we must choose wisely to continue."

"But how?" I asked, turning to them. "If this path was mistaken, then how do we proceed?"

Justice's gaze was steady. "The cards offer no simple truths or guarantees. The insights they provide are only as clear as the mind that perceives them."

"The only way forward," said Ximena, her voice calm but certain, "is with a new spread. I suggest the Celtic Cross. This spread will reveal not only your present dilemma but the true nature of your conflicts—their origins, your recent past, the best path forward, and the final resolution."

Justice nodded. "It is indeed a thorough course, though it may reveal truths that could be hard to face."

The Count approached me, his expression uncharacteristically tender as he placed a reassuring hand on my shoulder. "This will be difficult, Prince Aaron. Perhaps we should wait, give you time to rest before we embark on this journey."

I took a deep breath, feeling the weight of his words but also a renewed sense of clarity. "No," I said firmly. "Let us continue. I may not have all the answers, but I am ready to face whatever truths the cards reveal."

A quiet resolve settled over the room. Elder Anastasia began shuffling the deck anew, the sound of the cards a rhythmic whisper, as if they, too, held secrets waiting to be unveiled.

The Celtic Cross

The suggestion of a Celtic Cross reading resounded through the chamber, sparking animated discussions among the arcane figures. Each tarot character debated who would serve as the Significator—the central lens through which the intricate tapestry of my future would come into focus.

From the cards, the Four Knights emerged, each stepping onto the grand table where the tarot community had gathered. Shoulder to shoulder, they formed a formidable quartet, their voices uniting in perfect harmony.

"We shall continue to be his Significator," they declared in unison. "We will transcend any challenge for our Prince."

First to catch my eye was the Knight of Wands, his armor ablaze in fiery reds and golds, as though woven from strands of sunlight itself. He embodied audacity and action, an unstoppable force of ambition. Beside him stood the Knight of Cups, draped in shades of blue and silver, exuding tranquility and introspection. His presence softened the air, invoking reflection and emotional depth.

The Knight of Swords was wrapped in a shimmering, stormy aura, his armor a blend of silver and azure. His energy was a whirlwind of decisive thought and swift action, cutting through ambiguity with a single glance. Finally, the Knight of Pentacles, grounded and steadfast, emanated a quiet strength, a silent promise of stability and determination.

Each knight represented an essential aspect of my character—ambition, introspection, decisiveness, and endurance. Together, they formed a complete lens, a kaleidoscope of qualities through which my complex fate would be explored.

Elder Anastasia inclined her head approvingly as the knights took their places, asserting their role as my Significators. Their overlapping voices painted a symphony of contrasting melodies—valor, emotional depth, swift judgment, and quiet resilience—all resonating as aspects of my own nature. A sense of awe filled me; I felt fortified by their collective strength.

Just then, a wave of fatigue swept over me. The incense grew overwhelmingly potent, and my vision blurred. Rising from my seat, I tried to steady myself, but my legs gave way. The room spun, and I fell, hitting the ground hard as a flash of pain erupted in my head.

"Prince Aaron, are you alright?" Count Corvin knelt by my side, his face etched with concern.

"I'm fine," I mumbled, attempting to regain composure. "Just a bit tired. Let's continue."

"Perhaps he should rest," Ximena interjected, her tone firm. "He seems too fatigued to proceed."

Count Corvin glanced at the others before making his decision. "Matt, escort Prince Aaron to his quarters and ensure he is not disturbed."

"Yes, Count," Matt replied, helping me to my feet and guiding me from the chamber.

The dim corridor felt strangely comforting as we made our way to my quarters. Once inside, Matt helped me ease into my coffin bed, a luxurious sarcophagus lined with dark red velvet. For a moment, I allowed myself to sink into the cushions, my mind spinning with fragments of memories.

"Aaron, you must remember who you are," Ximena's voice interrupted my thoughts. "This place, it isn't truly living."

"But I'm content here," I protested. "There's no stress, no conflict. I've found peace by Count Corvin's side. Matt is my family now."

Ximena's eyes narrowed. "Matt is your servant, not your kin. This life is a gilded cage. What if you regain your memories too late to return to the world that's waiting for you?"

"I'll cross that bridge when I come to it. Let me enjoy the peace I have now."

Her gaze softened but remained resolute. "Aaron, this isn't peace; it's avoidance. You've forgotten what it feels like to live freely. To feel the sunlight on your skin, to face life unshielded. This existence isn't a life—it's a shadow of one."

I felt a surge of defiance. "I am content, Ximena," I insisted. "Everything I need is provided here."

At that moment, a distant bell echoed through the room.

"That bell is for you, Master," Matt murmured, his eyes filled with quiet concern.

"Then let's continue the reading," I said, sitting up, determined to prove that my memories would return on their own terms. Producing a faded photograph, Ximena handed it to me, her fingers lingering for a moment as if reluctant to let go.

"That's you," she whispered, her voice almost a plea.

I studied the image—a family gathered together, their faces familiar yet distant. But as I gazed at the photograph, a sense of recognition stirred within me, and a flicker of memory began to take shape.

"I'll try," I said quietly, my voice laced with uncertainty.

The journey back to the chamber felt heavier this time, as though the weight of my forgotten past clung to my steps. When I reentered, Count Corvin was waiting, his eyes meeting mine with unwavering intensity. He extended his hand, guiding me back to my seat.

"My Prince, it is time," he said, his tone reverent.

I took a deep breath, nodding. "Let the reading commence."

With the four knights as my Significators, I felt prepared to delve into the mysteries awaiting me, the Celtic Cross spread lying before us like an uncharted map of my soul.

Role of The Present Situation

Elder Anastasia sat at the far end of an intricately carved wooden table, her gaze both piercing and gentle, never straying from the tarot spread before her.

"Who will assume control over the present situation?" she asked.

A figure materialized beside the cards. "I am the Wheel of Fortune," declared an androgynous figure with flowing silver hair, their form a mesmerizing blend of light and shadow. They cradled an ornate wheel adorned with symbols and radiant gemstones, each spin mirroring the cosmos turning.

"The current state is clear to us," they began, their incandescent eyes locking onto mine. "But you, Prince Aaron, remain blind to it. You are trapped in illusion, unable to discern reality from fiction. This denial has already cost you, and it will continue to do so."

Elder Anastasia smiled faintly, her eyes glancing toward me with a mix of understanding and challenge.

The Wheel continued. "You live within a construct of your own making, confusing it for the world. You dismiss the emotions guiding you, unaware that even your will is bound to a larger design. This wheel represents life's unending cycles—the rise and fall of circumstances, the chain of choices and consequences."

"Embrace it, Prince Aaron," they whispered.

Compelled, I reached for the wheel. As my fingers made contact, a surge of energy pulsed through me, and my eyelids grew heavy. Suddenly, I was adrift in a dreamscape, worlds collapsing and reforming around me, their arcs woven from threads of love, pain, pleasure, and loss. A tapestry of life itself unfurled before me, real and yet undeniably illusory.

When I awoke, the figure was gone, leaving Elder Anastasia alone at the table. But something within me felt changed, as if the veils concealing my understanding had lifted, and I saw life in sharper clarity. The Wheel of Fortune had spun, and I was irrevocably altered.

I EMERGED FROM MY DREAM-filled rest with new clarity, remnants of the previous night's reading still lingering. Pushing open the lid of my coffin, its hinges creaking, I saw Matt, my faithful servant, standing nearby.

"Master, did you rest well?" he asked, his voice gentle.

"I did, Matt. I feel... renewed." Stretching my limbs, I felt an unusual vitality coursing through me. "And you—how are you this morning?"

Matt shifted, eyes averting slightly. "I am well, Master."

As I stepped onto the plush carpet, my gaze fell on him. "What happened to your ear?"

"Nothing, Master. I accidentally bumped into something in the kitchen," he replied, though I sensed discomfort in his tone.

"Show me."

Reluctantly, Matt turned, revealing raw, red lines on his back, like lash marks.

"Did Günter do this?" I asked, my voice tight.

"Yes, Master," he admitted softly. "I overslept last night. It was my own fault."

"It was unwarranted, and I will address it." I motioned for him to sit, carefully tending to his wounds. "For now, rest."

After a brief reprieve, he helped me bathe and dress, the soothing lavender-scented water easing the tensions of the night. The soft velvet of my robe draped around me as we made our way to the kitchen.

"What would you like for supper tonight, my Prince?" the Count asked, his voice warm.

"Sushi," I replied, savoring the thought of fresh fish and sharp wasabi.

The Count clapped his hands, and the kitchen staff began their preparations. The Count then handed me a newspaper. "You shouldn't keep yourself entirely cut off from the world."

I skimmed the headlines, setting the paper aside. "The same stories as ever—nations at war, needless bloodshed, the idle affairs of celebrities. It's all repetition."

The Count chuckled. "You are wise, my Prince."

And so, our day unfolded—a familiar rhythm, each action woven into the shared melody of our existence. Yet the words of the Wheel lingered, haunting me with their truth: my life was on the edge of transformation, poised between beginnings and endings.

AS DUSK FELL, WE RODE through the forest, twilight painting the sky in hues of violet and indigo. The rhythmic thud of our horses' hooves mingled with the night's stillness, a quiet communion of spirit between myself and the Count.

"My Prince, will you ever wish to journey beyond these woods with me?" he asked, his gaze thoughtful.

"I'm content here, Count. I see the world through your eyes, and that is enough."

He sighed, glancing toward the darkening trees. "You cannot stay here forever. It isn't right."

"For now, it is," I replied. "The world outside holds no allure."

At that moment, as if called by his words, the wheel from my reading appeared between us, spinning silently before tumbling to the forest floor. The androgynous figure from the Wheel of Fortune materialized to retrieve it, their voice echoing through the trees.

"You have neither a past nor a future. Your existence lies in a suspended present. If you wish to forge a future, you must first reclaim your past."

As their figure faded, I turned to the Count, but words escaped me.

"Does any of this resonate with you, my Prince?" he asked gently.

"Not yet," I replied, though doubt clouded my heart. Was I so trapped in my present that I'd forgotten to even seek my own past?

Our hands found each other in the quiet. We rode deeper into the forest, leaving my thoughts tangled in the mystery of the Wheel's message, feeling as though it had set me on a path toward truths still hidden.

"AARON, PLEASE COME back to us," Ximena's voice shattered my reverie, her plea striking a chord deep within. Memories and faces flashed through my mind, half-remembered fragments of another life.

"What do you mean, Ximena?" I asked, confusion tightening around me.

"Return to your family, to your true home," she urged. "In your search for answers, you've drifted too far."

"Is it not my right to seek understanding?" I countered. "Must I always abide by expectations and tradition?"

"It is, but not at the cost of those who love you—not at the cost of yourself," she replied gently.

"And if I cannot find my way back? Has the path home been changed by the journey?"

"Then we'll forge a new one," she said. "A wanderer may find much, but the deepest discoveries are often within those waiting for his return."

Her words seemed to open a window within me, revealing a forgotten light. "Your words bring me clarity, Ximena, a reminder of where I came from and where I belong."

"Then come back to us, Aaron. Battle your doubts. Find your way back to the heart of who you are."

IN THE END, THE WHEEL of Fortune had spun, opening doors to a past I'd left uncharted and a future beckoning from beyond. And for the first time, I saw a path—back to those who waited, a family, a home, and perhaps, a rediscovery of myself.

Role of The Issue At Hand

Elder Anastasia sat behind a worn oak table at the center of the mystical space, tarot cards spread before her like windows into other realms, each figure trembling with life.

"Who will step forward to address the matter at hand—the challenge that must be overcome?" Her voice, commanding yet measured, filled the room.

A radiant light emanated from the darkened corners of the chamber. Emerging with a celestial glow, a woman stepped forward. Her form was unclad, but an aura of purity enveloped her, golden hair flowing effortlessly behind her, a serene beauty etched across her face.

"I am The Star, and I shall undertake this challenge," she declared.

She held an ornate vessel containing a small sailing ship, tilting it so deliberately that time itself seemed to stretch, allowing its water to pour not as a puddle but as a shimmering mist, rising up to encircle me in a cool, refreshing aura.

"The issue before us is straightforward," she began, locking her tranquil gaze upon mine. "The Count yearns for an eternal love, one that transcends time and endures through the ages. Your generosity, your forgiveness, and your attentiveness have elevated him into a version of himself he scarcely believed possible."

I felt exposed yet enriched, as though The Star had unraveled a hidden tapestry of my life and held it up for me to witness. Love had orchestrated this cosmic dance in its most mystical form, inviting me to enter into an exquisitely promising future.

THE READING ROOM WAS a sanctuary of knowledge, with towering shelves laden with ancient tomes and modern works neatly aligned in dark mahogany. Sunlight streamed through the arched windows, spilling over the intricate oriental rug beneath us. The air smelled of old parchment and freshly brewed tea.

I sat at a writing desk, an antique piece that seemed to resonate with the scholarly pursuits of countless souls before me. My eyes skimmed across a manuscript, though my concentration faltered when the Count's voice broke the silence. His presence always filled any space.

"Aaron, what is your desire?" he asked.

I met his gaze.

"Ultimate happiness," I replied.

"As do I," he said. "We are united in this quest. What more does life hold for you?"

"To be exclusively with you," I answered without hesitation.

"You stand apart from other men I've known. Some sought wealth, others pursued power, and a few craved both. Others even desired to traverse the world."

"I covet none of that. My sole aspiration is to share my life with you," I assured him.

"Numerous souls have perished, craving beyond my offerings. Have you seen the grand tapestries adorning the corridors?" he asked.

"I have. They are exquisite artworks."

"Each commemorates a departed lover. Each reveals the demise these lovers faced while entwined with me."

"What do you mean?" I asked, feeling a pang of curiosity.

"Come, I will show you."

We rose from our chairs and exited the room, walking down the grand hallway. Once again, I was struck by the richness of the estate's decor—sumptuous red and gold wallpaper mingling with tapestries that told tales of love and loss. We stopped at the first of these woven artworks: a young man scrambling for coins at the Count's feet.

"This youth used me for my wealth," the Count explained. "He had no intentions beyond financial gain, offering companionship in exchange for money. He died impoverished and alone."

We moved to the next tapestry. The Count sat on a throne, a crown on his head, while a chained attendant knelt at his feet.

"He lusted for power?" I asked.

"Correct," the Count affirmed. "He craved dominion. His eyes were set on my lands, seeking to enslave those who had served me loyally for centuries."

"How did he meet his end?" I asked.

"His own slaves revolted, leading a mutiny that ended in his gruesome stoning."

"Master, why did you choose companions who mistreated you? I vow never to treat you in such a manner," I said, my voice filled with concern.

The Count paused, his eyes meeting mine with an intensity that sent a shiver through me.

"Indeed, My Prince, you have treated me with dignity and respect, which is why our destinies may be entwined."

We continued along the hallway, the Count recounting the stories behind each tapestry. Each narrative, though morose, served as a cautionary tale—a stark reminder of the perils that befell those who misunderstood or underestimated the profound nature of our bond.

As I listened, I grew more certain that my place beside the Count was destined, guided by a transcending force. Perhaps this very force would bring us the ultimate happiness we both sought.

THE ROOM WAS BATHED in a celestial glow as the Tarot characters seemed to come alive, their ethereal presence filling the space.

"The core of the issue lies in his refusal to confront reality," declared The Star, her voice ringing out clear and true, like a bell. "He mistakes truth for fiction. His perception is clouded by delusion, entangled in a web of his own making."

Her eyes locked onto mine with unwavering intensity.

"Resolving this matter requires self-acknowledgment. Aaron must disentangle himself from falsehoods and face the truth—raw and unfiltered."

Her words hung in the air, heavy with meaning.

Suddenly, another voice cut through the stillness like a shard of glass.

"Aaron, I implore you to recall your identity. Your life may be the next to be sacrificed," Ximena's voice echoed.

The Star, her purpose fulfilled, drifted back into the assembly with ethereal grace.

"Ximena, what do you mean?" I asked, confusion swirling in my chest. "How would my life be the next sacrificed?"

"Do you not see, Aaron?" Ximena's gaze pierced me. "The Count's history is a series of tragedies, leading to the demise of all his lovers. The Star speaks of confronting reality—your reality. You, too, must face the stark truth of entangling your destiny so completely with his."

Her words struck me like a lightning bolt. I felt as though a veil had been lifted, exposing a terrifyingly uncertain future. Would my tale be woven into the tapestry of the Count's sorrow-laden history? Would my face become another piece of artwork memorializing another tragic episode in his endless pursuit of ultimate happiness?

It was a haunting realization—but also a clarifying one. My journey ahead would be fraught with peril. Still, with the clarity of this mystical assembly, I felt prepared to navigate it. The stars had aligned to shed light on my path, challenging me to confront reality, embrace my true self, and move forward with courage and caution.

Role of The Root Of The Issue

Elder Anastasia's gaze swept over the living tarot cards assembled before her. Her voice, steady and clear, cut through the murmurs.

"Who will assume the role of addressing the core issue at hand?"

The earth trembled, and a sulfurous, acrid cloud erupted. When the air cleared, a strikingly handsome figure stood before us. It was Patrick, his face an enigma of charm and veiled intentions.

"Aaron, it's good to see you again," he said, his voice carrying a haunting familiarity. He was tall, his blond hair shimmering like threads of gold, and his blue eyes piercing. Clad in a half-buttoned red cowboy shirt, snug jeans, and spurred boots, he looked as if he had walked straight off the pages of a dream or a haunting memory.

Patrick strode toward me, each step resonating in the chamber. He reached out, clasping my hand in a firm, warm grasp, then led me to the center of the room, now transformed into a dance floor as a haunting melody began to play. He guided me effortlessly through the steps, leading me in a waltz of fate. But just as the final strains of music faded, Patrick pulled me close and, with shocking force, slapped me across the face. The blow sent me sprawling to the floor, a burning sting on my cheek, followed by the cold bite of handcuffs around my wrists.

"I am what you desire most in life," he declared.

"I am the Devil, here to reveal the root of all that binds you."

From the floor, I realized I could easily unlock the handcuffs; they were flimsy, almost begging to be undone. But I chose to remain bound, feeling their weight as a physical manifestation of my emotional and psychological burdens.

Patrick loomed over me, his gaze cutting into mine.

"You yearn for direction and freedom, but life defies simplicity. You have the choice: release your fears, let go, and embrace a life of light—or cling to them and descend into darkness."

As I lay there, handcuffed yet paradoxically free, I understood the depth of the choice before me—a path that could lead either to salvation or self-destruction.

"Release him and take your place," Ximena's voice cut through the air.

"I can't release him, Ximena. I love him, and he loves me," I shot back, meeting her gaze with defiance.

Ximena seated herself beside me, her voice both soft and firm.

"Aaron, can't you see? He has no power over you. It's all an illusion."

She hesitated, searching my face for understanding.

"Patrick has his own life, his own family. You're trapped in a prison of loneliness and longing."

The echoing footsteps of Count Corvin approached, his presence filling the room with authority. His cologne hung heavy in the air.

"Ximena, step away from him, or you will pay the price," he warned, his tone menacing.

Justice stepped between them, her form graceful yet unyielding.

"Count Corvin, let them be. Only she can guide him now."

The Count hesitated, his glare softened by reluctant acquiescence. He retreated, leaving Ximena and me in a space charged with unspoken truths. My mind wrestled with emotions—love, loneliness, freedom, and bondage. Was Patrick and the hold he had on me all just an illusion?

"I can't abandon him, Ximena," I confessed. "He's the foundation I've built my life upon. He soothes my soul."

"He's the source of your torment, can't you see? You're not in love with him; you're in love with an illusion, a distorted image of what love should be," Ximena insisted, her voice thick with empathy.

Tears blurred my vision.

"No one else has ever loved me the way Patrick did," I choked out.

Ximena took my hand, her grip both gentle and grounding.

"You've closed yourself off to the love others have offered. Many have tried to love you, but your vision is clouded by illusions of a love that could never be. Rise, Aaron, and free yourself from this deception."

I looked back at Patrick—or rather, the devil disguised as him. At that moment, I saw clearly. It wasn't Patrick holding me captive; it was my own insecurities and fears, a version of myself reflected in him.

"Can't you see?" Ximena whispered her voice like a balm. "You're shackled not by him but by your own illusions. Free yourself and embrace life."

With her arms around me, I rose, feeling as though a weight had been lifted. The chains were imaginary, yet their absence felt liberating. Ximena leaned in, pressing a reassuring kiss on my cheek.

"Let's end this illusion. You're back, Aaron," Ximena said softly, her voice a promise of release.

But the threads of the illusion lingered.

"I'm still uncertain. I remember Patrick's proposal," I murmured.

Ximena's eyes narrowed, disbelief flickering across her face.

"You cannot be serious!"

Justice moved to separate us gently.

"He must confront his memories, Ximena."

Count Corvin led me to the throne, a regal structure adorned with intricate filigree and deep crimson upholstery.

"Tell us, Aaron, how did he propose to you?"

"No!" Ximena cried out, but Justice held her back.

And so, I began recounting the story of Patrick's proposal, peeling back layers of an illusion that had long ensnared me.

"We were gathering supplies for the school dance at the shopping center," I began, the memory unfolding in my mind like a dream.

"He took the keys in the parking lot and knelt down, looking into my eyes. 'Aaron, will you marry me?' he asked, and I said 'Yes,' almost without thinking. We'd only been together for three months, but it felt so real. I wanted to believe I was in love."

The room was silent. Every face turned toward me. The memory felt heavy, like a stone resting on my chest.

"How did it end?" the Devil asked, his eyes gleaming.

"Six months later, after a night of what I thought was intimacy, he told me he was 'going back to women,'" I whispered, the words thick with pain. "He said it casually as if he were discussing the weather."

The Devil grinned, a twisted echo of the Patrick I thought I knew.

"And the next morning, I still made him breakfast. I even did his laundry. I ran into Doug, my closest friend, at the laundromat. I confessed, 'He's going back to women,' feeling nothing but shame."

The memory pressed down on me, suffocating.

"And when we returned, Patrick asked Doug for a favor. Doug, my confidant, the one person I thought I could trust, knelt before Patrick and... gratified him while I watched, stunned and shattered."

The room held its collective breath, the intensity of my revelation heavy in the air.

Ximena finally broke the silence.

"Don't you see, Aaron? You were enchanted by words, ensnared by false promises. You accepted a distorted love to avoid facing the emptiness within yourself."

The Devil shifted, his form reverting back to Patrick's familiar guise.

"This was all an illusion, Aaron. Not everything you see or hear is true. Embrace the reality of your existence."

With a final swirl of acrid smoke, he disappeared, leaving me alone on the throne. Tears streaked down my face, each one a testament to years of self-deception. How could I have been so blind?

As the smoke cleared, I felt a stirring—a small, tentative seed of clarity. My journey was far from over, but at last, I was beginning to see the light through the illusion.

Role of The Recent Past Events

Seated behind an antiquated oak table laden with esoteric trinkets and a well-worn Tarot deck, Elder Anastasia adjusted her shawl. Her gaze was steady as she addressed the gathering.

"Who will assume the role of Recent Past Events?" she asked, her voice both commanding and curious.

A figure detached himself from the assembly.

"I, The Chariot, shall take on the mantle of Recent Past Events," he proclaimed.

Clad in a pilot's uniform reminiscent of a bygone era of monumental wars and mechanical innovation, he cut a dashing figure. A precisely groomed mustache graced his upper lip, and his short brown hair was hidden beneath a cap adorned with various insignia—badges of honor and valor. His aviator glasses obscured his eyes, adding a layer of mystery to his presence.

With an air of quiet authority, he strode toward me, his leather boots hitting the stone floor in sync with the crackling firelight and whispered murmurs of the tarot characters. As he reached me, he carefully removed his aviator glasses and placed them in my hand.

"These are more than mere glasses, Prince Aaron," he intoned, meeting my gaze with a look both fierce and wise. "They represent the vision you have gained through recent trials, battles fought not just with steel but with spirit. You have emerged victorious, yet remember: The Chariot warns against hubris. Do not forget the sacrifices that brought you here, nor the steady hand that has guided you forward."

His words resonated deeply. The past wasn't a mere shadow trailing behind me; it was the very foundation I now stood upon. The weight of his glasses in my hand felt like a link to all I'd endured and achieved—the battles won, the lessons learned, the scars, and the triumphs that marked my journey.

Elder Anastasia nodded approvingly. Clutching the aviator glasses, I felt a new appreciation for all that The Chariot represented: a chapter in my life that had shaped me, now guiding me into whatever lay in the House of Ideas.

THE BAR WAS SOAKED in nostalgia, and its vintage decor and eclectic crowd created an ambiance that was both intimate and loud. Maria and I settled into a padded leather booth at Finnegan's, a local spot known for its classic charm. Soft jazz floated from unseen speakers, filling the room with a mellow hum, while the neon glow of signs bathed the exposed brick walls in warm colors. Glasses clinked, conversations swelled, and the smell of sizzling appetizers mingled with the hint of whiskey.

"What's got you so worked up tonight?" Maria asked, narrowing her eyes as she sipped her gin and tonic.

"Another round with Ximena," I sighed, fingers tracing the side of my Old Fashioned.

"What's the fight about this time?"

I shrugged, glancing down at my fiery red blazer. "The same old story. Ximena insists I don't have a life because I'm always fussing over Mom."

Maria tilted her head, looking at my blazer with a smirk. "And is the red blazer a statement or just tonight's fashion choice?"

"More of a statement," I admitted. "A sartorial expression of my inner chaos, maybe."

Maria chuckled. "So, why red?"

"Because it feels like fire—me and Ximena are just two flames burning each other out."

She shook her head. "I don't get why you two clash so much. She's practically become your sparring partner in this never-ending family drama."

"She thinks she can drift through life because she's younger. Meanwhile, I'm supposed to stay rooted, taking care of Mom. I'm the eldest and, according to her, doomed to be the caretaker."

Maria set her drink down, leveling me with a serious look. "Aaron, you need to go live your own life. You're too old to still be living at home, waiting for something or someone to change. Don't you think?"

"Wait—are you taking her side now?" I shot back, the disbelief clear in my voice.

"No, I'm taking your side," Maria replied, unfazed. "But you've got to admit, you're using family obligations as a shield. And Patrick, too. Your unrequited love and your family dynamics are keeping you from finding something real."

"I'm not hiding," I said, a bit defensively.

"Really? Because from where I stand, you're still hung up on Patrick. You're letting a decade-old age gap between you and Ximena and Santino be an excuse for why you can't move forward."

Her words hit harder than I expected. I realized she wasn't wrong—whether it was the red blazer, my constant clashes with Ximena, or my lingering feelings for Patrick, they were all symptoms of a life lived halfway, a life waiting for a spark that could only be ignited from within.

It was time, I realized, to stop letting the past and others' expectations define me.

Role of The Best Solution

"Who will rise to the occasion as the best solution in this predicament?" Elder Anastasia's voice, calm yet resonant, cut through the atmosphere heavy with expectation. Her gaze was steady as it moved over the spread of Tarot cards, then lifted to the room.

"I, The Emperor, shall take charge," boomed a voice that seemed to rumble from the very stones beneath us.

A man, stout and imposing, positioned himself beside me. Though his bearing demanded attention, it was undercut by an air of vanity. His slicked-back hair, an unremarkable shade of gold, was topped with an elaborate crown encrusted with jewels, each gem catching the light and seeming to shout for notice.

"You would lead us, Emperor?" I asked, raising an eyebrow. "What do you propose?"

The Emperor smiled, his teeth slightly yellowed. "I propose strength, young prince. I propose a rule that bends to neither whimsy nor superstition. Leadership demands a firm hand."

My eyes narrowed. "And if strength turns to tyranny? An Emperor may rule, but even he is subject to the consequences of his choices."

"Tyranny is a word used by those who misunderstand the need for control," he replied.

I glanced over at Elder Anastasia, whose expression remained impassive, her hands resting gently on the cards. The Emperor was both structure and authority—qualities necessary for order, yet dangerous if left unchecked.

"Very well," I said, my tone even, "but know this: strength without wisdom is a ship without a compass. It may float, but it will not find its way to any worthy destination."

The Emperor chuckled. "Then let us hope, Prince Aaron, that I am as wise as I am strong."

DAREN PULLED INTO THE gas station, the car vibrating with anticipation as he parked beside a fuel pump. "Just an hour until the party. It's going to be unforgettable!" he said, his voice full of excitement.

"I need the restroom," I said, climbing out of the car and heading toward the building. The crunch of gravel underfoot mixed with the distant hum of traffic. I felt the adrenaline of the night building.

In the restroom, a sudden wave of darkness overwhelmed me. My head spun as I blinked, trying to regain my bearings. When my senses returned, I was no longer at the gas station. I was bound at the corners of a wooden table, my wrists and ankles stretched painfully. The air was thick with the scent of mold, damp wood, and an unsettling sweetness I couldn't identify.

"Just stay still," a voice drawled. A young man loomed over me, his expression both curious and predatory. He held a pill between his teeth and leaned down, pressing it onto my lips with his own, forcing it into my mouth with a disturbing intimacy.

"Who are you?" I managed, my mind racing. "What's going on?"

He smirked, his breath sickly sweet. "Just relax. You'll enjoy what I have in store."

Footsteps echoed down the hall, and a voice—thick with a German accent—called out. "Junior, are you down here?"

Junior's expression darkened. "Yes, Father, I have our guest prepared as an offering for the Count."

I froze, a sick realization dawning on me. I'd stumbled into a nightmare. The anticipation of the party was now a distant memory, drowned by the horror of this place.

Junior's father entered, his presence like a dark cloud. The scent of alcohol wafted from him as he leaned in close to his son. "We won't let you become the Count's companion," he murmured, casting a cold glance at me. "Let him take this one instead."

Junior hesitated. "But Father, I've avoided the Count for so long. I don't mind meeting him."

Gunter's eyes hardened. "No, Junior. The Count doesn't need to know who you are. Give this man to him. He's younger than he looks."

I clenched my teeth, anger simmering beneath my fear. "I'm not here for any of this."

But Gunter ignored me. "Junior, prepare him with this." He handed his son a chalice filled with a murky liquid. "Give him this to drink—it will erase his memory. Then leave him for the Count."

The chalice was pushed into my line of sight, and I fought against the urge to comply, my mind screaming to resist.

THE EMPEROR'S CHAMBER was as grand as it was oppressive. Towering alabaster pillars reached up to an intricately painted ceiling, where celestial scenes played out in rich, gilded patterns. The polished marble floor mirrored the flickering candlelight, casting a thousand shadows in the vast space.

Clad in a royal purple robe embroidered with gold, the Emperor sat upon a jade throne, a fortress of cold authority. He looked down at me, his expression hard as stone.

"The most fitting solution here," he declared, "is for this man to release himself from these imagined attachments. He's surrounded himself with enemies masquerading as friends. His task is to recognize these ties for what they are—a trap of his own making."

His words, heavy as they were, felt like a final pronouncement of my past. They sought to reshape my very being.

The Emperor rose and exited the chamber, leaving behind the faintest echo of his words.

Ximena stepped forward, her gaze fierce as she addressed the Count. "Aaron is not the one bound to your fate by prophecy. Release him."

But the Count didn't so much as flinch.

Justice, a towering figure draped in a robe of silver and blue, moved to Ximena's side. He laid a hand on her shoulder, his voice calm yet firm. "The Count does not yield to emotional pleas, Lady Ximena."

In the flickering light, I stood torn between them, caught in the gravity of choices I hadn't yet made, yet felt on the brink of understanding.

Role of The Next Step

Elder Anastasia's eyes glinted with a pearl of wisdom as old as the rituals themselves. She asked, "Who will assume the next pivotal role?"

Her voice floated through the chamber, thick with the scent of incense and the unspoken reverence of ages past. From the shadows stepped a figure of quiet yet mesmerizing beauty: The Priestess.

Her raven-black hair flowed like a waterfall, dark strands stark against the moonlit white of her garment, which seemed spun from clouds themselves. Her piercing gaze met mine, steady and knowing.

"I am The Priestess, and I shall guide Aaron from here." Her voice was soft yet authoritative, a calm breeze brushing over troubled waters.

Reaching out, she took my hand, her touch light yet electrifying, and led me to Ximena, who had been watching from the edge of the room.

"Take him to Manuel and ensure his well-being," The Priestess instructed.

Ximena wrapped her arm around mine and navigated me through the curious throng until we reached my chamber, where Manuel was already pacing. He turned toward me with eyes filled with anticipation.

"Brother, you're here! Does this mean we can finally go home?" His words tumbled out breathlessly.

I felt the weight of conflicting desires press on my heart. "Not yet," I replied slowly. "The Priestess advised us to come to you." I was acutely aware of Ximena's gaze, measuring my every reaction.

Ximena's voice broke the silence, firm and resolute. "Aaron, you can't just let others dictate your choices. You have to exercise your own will."

"I'm at a crossroads," I admitted. "Letting go of Patrick wasn't easy, and what if I don't want to remember everything?"

Ximena's expression hardened. "You should retain some memories," she said quietly.

"I remember the arguments about Mother," I responded, the memories trickling back like water through cracks in a dam.

"It's more than that, Aaron. We've never seen you in a committed relationship. If you keep avoiding this, you might end up carrying all the responsibility for Mother."

As she spoke, a wave of memories rose within me. The weight of that looming future was heavily uncertain. But would I find my way? Only time, that most unyielding of judges, would tell.

I shifted my focus to Manuel, searching his face. "And what about you, Manuel? You haven't been in a serious relationship for a while, either. Why isn't Ximena urging you to care for Mother?" My words had an edge, the frustration barely masked.

Manuel held my gaze, undeterred. "Because I've built a life, Aaron. I have a job, a home, and yes, I'm dating." His voice was tinged with defensiveness yet laced with honesty.

Ximena stepped forward, her youthful indignation palpable. "I'm only nineteen! It's not fair to expect so much from me."

"I know," I sighed, looking down, "and Santino is only seventeen." The words hung in the air, heavy with the shared burdens we couldn't ignore.

After a pause, Manuel softened. "Take the next step, Aaron. Come home with us."

The silence grew deep until the chamber door creaked open, and the familiar scent of incense drifted in. The Priestess stood in the doorway, her dark eyes holding an invitation.

"It's time to return to the grand hall for the completion of the reading," she intoned.

Her words seemed to shift the very atmosphere. Our individual dilemmas would have to wait. With a sense of silent unity, we filed out of my chamber, drawn together by a single purpose: to return to the grand hall, to face Elder Anastasia, and to confront the cards that held fragments of my fate.

Role of How You'll Deal

The air in the grand hall was thick with incense and an aura of untold wisdom, every flickering shadow holding a secret. Heavy maroon curtains blocked out the afternoon light, casting the room in twilight. Golden candelabras stood in each corner, their dancing flames illuminating tapestries woven with stories older than memory itself. In the room's center, a table adorned with an embroidered cloth bore a spread of Tarot cards, a small bowl of water, and a scattering of timeworn runes.

Elder Anastasia, robed in celestial blue embroidered with golden symbols, sat in silent contemplation when a figure materialized from behind her. Radiant yet solemn, Justice stepped forward, her robes in hues of balanced grays and silver, a set of scales held steady in her hands.

"I've come to weigh how you're handling this," Justice declared, her voice a blend of calm authority. "Your family, your attachment to Patrick—they aren't the heart of the issue. There's something deeper, a truth you haven't yet acknowledged."

"Are you suggesting my family and loyalty are irrelevant?" I questioned, my tone wavering between defiance and vulnerability.

"Not irrelevant," she replied, her eyes meeting mine with an intensity that felt like a judgment. "But secondary. There is a truth, an unspoken reality that you've chosen to ignore."

Elder Anastasia, watching intently, interjected. "Justice appears to remind us of the balance we often overlook." She placed another card beside Justice. "Prince Aaron, this isn't the end of your journey, but a crucial turning point."

At that moment, the weight of the truth became almost tangible, pressing down on me. I felt the scales of Justice tipping as if waiting for me to release the illusions I clung to.

I KNOCKED ON RAMONA'S door. When she opened it, her face wore a heavy layer of red eyeliner and a smear of pink blush, a bold but vain attempt to defy the years. At thirty-five, her face held both strength and weariness, framed by a short, powerful figure.

"Hello, how are you?" she asked, her voice a curious mix of genuine warmth and a hint of mockery.

"Could be better," I replied, stepping inside. The stale air held a faint note of perfume over the unmistakable undertone of alcohol.

"Care for a beer?" She extended a can, her chipped red nails catching the dim light.

"You know I don't drink," I said, moving toward the worn sofa.

She scoffed, waving the can dismissively. "Oh, excuse me, 'Mr. I-Don't-Drink-Because-I-Was-Raped.'" She caught herself too late, regret flickering in her eyes.

"Really? We're doing this again?" I asked, disbelief and irritation creeping into my tone.

"I've been through things, too, and here I am," she said, popping the can open.

"Right, because I've yet to see you sober," I muttered, sarcasm shading my words.

She took a long sip, rolling her eyes. "So what's the issue this time?" she finally asked.

"I got fired," she replied, her voice faltering as she handed me a stack of paperwork. "They're saying I stole from the register."

I took the papers, glancing through them before drafting a clear, pointed response. "Here, this should help you make your case."

She nodded, a hint of gratitude in her eyes. "Thanks."

"You're welcome," I said. "But try not to get fired again."

She hesitated, then asked, "Ever thought about moving in here? With me?"

I avoided her gaze. "Not really."

"Aaron, your family isn't exactly loving. Here, you'd be free, even to have a boyfriend," she ventured.

"My family needs me, and in some way, I need them," I replied.

"For over a decade, I've told you: they don't care about you like I do. My divorce is final; you and I could marry, even with your... habits."

My head snapped up. "Marriage? You've never been faithful, so don't make me out to be a bigger mess than you are."

"My kids adore you. We're your real family," she pressed. "Your mother and the others have only ever tried to change you, haven't they?"

I faltered, torn. "I don't know, Ramona. I'm honestly not sure."

She handed me another beer, her fingers cold against mine. "Think about it. Maybe this will help."

We sat in a silence that was both bitter and comfortable, each nursing our truths like wounds, knowing they might never fully heal.

I TURNED TO XIMENA, who was watching me with barely concealed disdain.

"I can't stand that woman," she spat. "She's selfish and toxic. Why do you even talk to her?"

"Ximena, what you see as negativity could be her way of surviving," I countered.

"She's sabotaged you, Aaron, holding you back in ways you can't even see," Ximena replied, her voice sharp. "And you're clinging to her like a lifeline while she drags you down."

"I'm used to playing the victim, to be honest. I don't know my next move," I admitted.

Elder Anastasia's soft voice broke the tension. "We must continue the reading. These choices aren't simple," she said, her hands hovering over the deck.

As her fingers brushed the cards, I knew the next draw wasn't just another symbol—it was the next chapter of my life unfolding, with every raw truth I'd avoided waiting just on the other side.

The Outcome

"Who will take the place of individuals or events that will influence the outcome?" Elder Anastasia's voice hung in the air like a bell, filling the room's dense silence.

A woman stepped forward, shimmering in a golden robe adorned with jewels, the scent of roses trailing behind her like a whisper.

"Aaron, come back home," she implored, her voice carrying a mixture of longing and authority.

"Mother, I am here, but home is not where I feel complete," I replied.

"Your siblings need you," she said gently. "Your presence matters."

I closed my eyes, trying to find words through the tangle of emotions. "This reading has only brought back memories I'd rather forget. Family is both a gift and a curse."

"But we came here to bring you home," Ximena insisted.

"I never asked you to follow me," I said, fighting the urge to lash out. "I left to find myself, away from expectations, away from the weight of duty."

"Mother yearns for you," Ximena said softly.

"Our mother needs to live her life, to find herself without relying on me," I retorted. "She has you, Manuel, and Santino. She doesn't need to keep turning to me."

"We want you with us," Manuel interjected.

"No. You want someone to shoulder the burdens you're unwilling to carry," I countered. "I have my own life to lead."

"That's not true," Ximena said, defiance hardening her voice.

"Then leave before I ask Günter to lock you in the dungeon," I warned.

"You wouldn't dare," she challenged, her eyes narrowing.

Just then, my mother's voice cut through the tension. "My son, I regret your distress. But you must choose—will you stay with the Count, or will you come with us?"

I turned to the Count, taking his hands, feeling both gratitude and melancholy. "You've shown me kindness; you've offered me a sanctuary, but it is a world of shadows, a life frozen in time. I want to live—to experience mortality before anything eternal. Let me go."

The Count's gaze turned sorrowful. "I offered you freedom from pain, from loss," he whispered, his words a mix of frustration and grief.

"You offered me oblivion," I replied gently. "I left one cage only to find another. I need something real."

The Count sighed, a sound both resigned and tender. "I have longed for your companionship, but I won't hold you here against your will."

As he released my hands, I felt the weight of our connection ease. I was no longer a lost prince seeking shelter, and he was no longer the all-powerful master of my destiny. We were simply two souls accepting our separate paths.

"JUNIOR IS YOUR INTENDED," I announced to the Count.

"Do not listen to him," Günter snapped, his face paling. The Count looked from me to Günter, then back, confusion and dawning realization crossing his face.

"Günter, explain yourself," the Count demanded.

Günter hesitated, torn between obedience and some hidden truth. Finally, he spoke. "Junior has always been suited to you, Master, in ways I could never be. He possesses qualities that complement you."

The Count looked at Junior, then at Günter, and finally back at me. "It seems fate has woven threads beyond our control," he murmured.

I took a deep breath, feeling a release as the last pieces fell into place. "When I arrived, Junior drugged and delivered me to you, hoping it would win your favor. It was Günter who intervened, taking me to the moat where you found me, dazed and lost."

Ximena stepped forward, confusion in her gaze. "But Aaron, why did you lose your memories?"

I met her eyes. "It was a side effect of a medication, meant to dull memories of... everything I wanted to escape." I paused, a sense of clarity settling over me. "That, mixed with whatever Junior had given me, created the perfect storm."

Manuel, who had been silent, couldn't hold back any longer. "You are something else!" he muttered, half exasperated, half relieved.

I smirked. "I've been called worse," I said, glancing back at the Count. "But today, I reclaim my life. I am Aaron—a son, a brother, a seeker of my own path."

"Master," I continued, "may we now depart and live as we choose?"

The Count's expression softened, and he nodded. "Yes, you are free. Your family will remain unharmed, and Matt may join you."

Günter's face twisted. "Matt's destiny lies with Junior, not with Aaron!" he objected.

I turned to Matt, who stood quietly, his face open and calm. "Matt, no one has the right to decide your path but you."

Matt gave me a small smile. "Thank you, Aaron. My path is my own, and I'll handle it in my own way."

I turned back to the Count, a sense of finality settling over me. "Please, protect Matt. Let him find his own happiness."

The Count placed a hand on my shoulder, nodding solemnly. "Matt will be safe, as will you."

I took one last look at the Count, his face tinged with sadness and acceptance, before turning to Elder Anastasia and Justice.

"Justice," I greeted her, bowing my head slightly. "Guide my family to their true paths. As for me, I choose to walk my own."

Justice's voice rang with quiet strength. "Your choice is yours alone. Walk with purpose, Prince Aaron."

My heart was full, and I turned to my siblings. "I may have been distant, but I see now that my place is with you. I'm sorry for all the years I failed to see the love you offered."

Ximena pulled me into a fierce hug. "We've missed you."

With that, I took her hand, ready to face whatever lay beyond. Together, we stepped through the door and into the dawn of a new beginning.

As I embraced the open world beyond the grand hall, I felt the weight of the past slip away. I had reclaimed my life, leaving behind illusions for the reality I had always deserved. I was free at last, walking forward, a future as boundless as the horizon ahead.

New Beginning

The air was thick with the scents of moss, damp earth, and fresh rain, as though the heavens themselves had washed the world clean in anticipation of our departure. The cobblestones beneath our feet, worn by countless travelers before us, glistened faintly under the muted light. The towering stone walls of the castle, which had once felt like an impenetrable fortress holding me captive, now appeared as relics of a past life I was leaving behind.

Justice, our guide and guardian, led Ximena, Manuel, and me across the courtyard, her steps assured and steady. She paused, turning to me with a rare, gentle smile.

"Are you ready, Aaron?" she asked.

I looked at her, then at my siblings beside me. "I've never been more certain of anything," I replied.

As we stepped through the grand archway to the world beyond, a horse-drawn carriage appeared as though summoned by our resolve. Its wooden frame was elegantly carved and gilded, a striking blend of strength and grace. The horses were almost regal, their manes gleaming. The driver—a middle-aged man in well-tailored attire—stood ready, his gaze steady and respectful.

"This will take you to the modern world," Justice said. "The transition may disorient you, but remember—you have each other."

I turned to Ximena and Manuel. "We'll face this new world together, and we'll create the life we've always wanted."

"And together, we'll return to our mother and Santino. Our family will be whole again," Ximena said, her voice firm and filled with hope.

Manuel clapped me on the back. "To new beginnings," he said.

"And to the end of false friendships and toxic associations," I added, a faint smile tugging at the corners of my mouth.

The carriage driver dismounted and opened the door, bowing slightly as he gestured for us to enter.

Justice inclined her head. "Step in, embrace your destiny, and fear not—I will always be with you, gently guiding you along the path meant for you."

"Thank you, Justice," I said, my voice filled with gratitude. "We are forever in your debt."

"Debt has no place in the life you're stepping into," she replied. "Go now—embrace your freedom."

One by one, we climbed into the carriage. As the door closed, a profound sense of finality settled over me, like the closing of a long chapter. I whispered, more to myself than to anyone else:

"Onward toward the life we are meant to live."

THE END

Don't miss out!

Visit the website below and you can sign up to receive emails whenever Andres Fragoso Jr publishes a new book. There's no charge and no obligation.

https://books2read.com/r/B-A-VNZS-BPIIF

BOOKS 2 READ

Connecting independent readers to independent writers.

Did you love *The Tarot Saga: Prince Aaron's Fate*? Then you should read *Under the Lemon Tree: a Family Recipe of Jealousy, Lies, and Betrayal*[1] by Andres Fragoso Jr!

Under the Lemon Tree is written on the same ideas of family. A book of poetry that tells the story of the Lemon Tree family. This book shows different personalities that changed themselves from good to bad, from heroes to villains. This is a story that almost everyone in the world can relate to because it happens to so many families. I have seen families torn apart by lies, cheating, stealing, and self-hate. This story is about seven beautiful sisters and a brother. The sisters ruin their family name and take everyone to the most profound decline. Their nephew, the story's protagonist, believed them to be divine. From childhood, he walked with them, followed them, and did whatever they did. They were like a goddess to him who could never make mistakes. He used to feel proud of them always. The family name, Lemon Tree, was turned from great respect to being the joke of the town. All the sisters fighting over an inheritance that

---

1. https://books2read.com/u/4Nj7vN

2. https://books2read.com/u/4Nj7vN

doesn't belong to them. They lied to each other and created misconceptions and misunderstandings. They gay-shamed their brother and nephew for being gay, for being men of culture and education, for being honest with themselves and no longer their puppets. The protagonist realizes how the sisters have abused them emotionally, verbally, and sometimes mentally. Under the lemon tree is a defining story from a colorful past relished under great, honorable, honest, and upright grandparents to a bitter family dispute that has ruined everything and everyone's life.

Read more at andresfragosojr.com.

About the Author

Andres Fragoso, Jr., is an author, blogger, freelance ghostwriter, journalist, mentor, poet, publicist, and much more. Loves to create new stories and has many ideas to write. In writing gay fiction, he shows the other aspects of being human in his works. Without dwelling on either issue, his characters come to life overcoming obstacles that are beyond their control. Andres has published many fiction and non-fiction books with many stories and poetry online, anthologies, and articles in various online magazines. "My mission in life is to help other authors and writers improve their craft. As I help them, they help me improve mine." Andres' experience comes from over 30 years in customer services, managing large and small corporations, and volunteering his time. He is in various writers groups, both online and in-person, such as Las Vegas Writers Group, Henderson Writers Group, Las Vegas Erotic Group, and Authors in Pajamas, Andres' current projects and clients include Friends of Dorothy Club, FIND, Fabulous Image, Wally Hawkins Photography, to name a few. Under his company name, The Ghoster. He is the author of Writer's Sidekick Series Notebooks published un Writer's Sidekick Publishing.

Read more at andresfragosojr.com.

About the Publisher

Writers Sidekick Publishing was established in 2021. To publish its Writers Sidekick Notebook Series. Notebooks that help guide writers to organize and keep track of their characters, settings, plot, and more.

Read more at www.writerssidekick.com.